Enc

of

Books

and other stories

Enchantress of Books

♦ ♦ ♦ and other stories ♦ ♦ ♦

ALISON MCBAIN

ISBN-13: 978-1-949122-12-1 (Paperback)
ISBN-13: 978-1-949122-13-8 (eBook)

Front cover art by Richard Ong.
Back cover image by Gerd Altmann.
Cover and interior design by Alison McBain.

Fairfield Scribes
Fairfield, CT
United States of America

First printing April 2019.

To Jeanne and Mike—
your support and love is all the magic I need.
Thank you, thank you, thank you.

Contents

♦ ♦ ♦ ENCHANTRESS OF ♦ ♦ ♦

Some people might say I've created lives. Some people might say I've destroyed them.

But I would be the first to admit: a choice like this really shouldn't have been given to me.

♦ ♦ ♦

"Susan—I'm sorry to do this to you. Ed turned in his story late and the book is about to go to press. I don't have time to edit it." My boss, Dave, thunked the hard copy down on my desk. I shared the space with two other co-workers, since budget cuts now extended to furniture. The *City Voice* *m*agazine—a "book" in industry speak—employed each editor only twenty hours a week. Because of my son's school schedule, I always took morning shift.

"You want me to edit Ed's story?" I hesitantly pushed up my glasses to take a look, but Dave walked away instead of answering me.

Our star writer Ed was a pain in the ass. Ed was old school . . . like the Dark Ages. He never let me touch his work, not after my first copyedit on the job had revealed he played fast and loose with his so-called facts. Ed had thrown a tantrum when I'd tried to point out his errors, and gone storming to management. Now, usually only Dave got the privilege of telling Ed when his "true" stories veered over into fiction.

But Dave already knew Ed's peculiarities, so if he gave me the story . . . it must be okay.

Ed's editorial hooked me at once, even though he played fast and loose with his comma choices. The story was about our city's former mayor, Julian James. He'd gotten caught up in fraud and embezzlement while in office; a common-enough tale. But his tale became unique when the investigating FBI agent disappeared. Although no body turned up, the ensuing scandal was massive and immediate. Even more so when James killed himself just days before charges were supposed to drop, with a highly publicized suicide "note" recorded on YouTube.

"Poor kid," I muttered to myself as I read the snippet of an interview with Julian's adult son. The guy was crying in the picture accompanying the article, his arm around his mother, James' widow. "Too bad it turned out the way it did. His dad really shouldn't have killed himself. Of course, James should've been smart enough to be on the right side of the law."

Ed's original story had skyrocketed to national fame, and this one-year follow-up piece was sure to draw widespread attention, too. Until Ed's story broke, there had been talk about shutting the magazine down. The old fart had saved all our jobs. It always made me wonder why Ed stayed at such a small nickel-and-dime mag. Even if all his contacts were local, I figured the good ol' boy network could hook him up on a national level. Or perhaps he was worried that the bigger books wouldn't take his BS accounting of facts.

I didn't exist to him, though. He once said "Hi, Brenda" to me after we'd worked together for two years. Since Brenda's a tall, skinny blonde and I'm a short, curvy brunette, it gave me a strong idea of my placement on his professional radar.

I edited and emailed the story off to Dave, then glanced at the clock. Sure enough, it was two minutes until I had to run to get my son, Bobby.

On the way out the door, I nearly collided with Dave. He seemed like he was struggling to speak, his expression best described as "needing to eat a bran muffin."

I gave him a half-wave, but didn't wait for him to collect his thoughts. Bobby got antsy if I was late, even by a few minutes. I loved him to bits, but I figured the teachers already had their hands full with him during the day.

I prayed that my old Honda wouldn't be temperamental. I was in luck; after an initial chug and cough, the rusty vehicle shuddered to life. I made it to school with thirty seconds to spare. When Bobby came out the door, his face lit up as soon as he saw me—not "too cool" to be happy to see mom. We went hand-in-hand to the car and, miracle of miracles, the Honda started on the first try.

Bobby was like a parakeet, constantly chirping until we got to our one-bedroom apartment. It took a while to settle him down to working on his first-grade homework, and my help mostly consisted of reminding him to focus. After a couple of TV shows, we ate dinner and I tucked him into bed with twenty kisses, one for each finger and toe (our ritual since he was a baby). I stayed up late doing a few freelance editing projects—making ends meet editing teens' school papers, college essays, and Suzy Homemaker blog articles. Until the words started to blur. On the sixth read-through of the same sentence on how to sautée onions, I pulled out the sleeper sofa and fell onto it.

For some reason, my alarm blared me awake fifteen minutes later than normal. Had I accidentally reset it or hit the snooze button? I rolled out of bed and took a shower in lightning time. When I hit the kitchen to microwave yesterday's old coffee on the way to wake Bobby, I stopped dead. On the counter was a brand-new, single-cup coffeemaker.

I'd always wanted one, but they were expensive, especially for the k-cups. Much more pricey than the usual pot and scoop. Sleep deprivation didn't equal new appliances, as far as I knew. How had this gotten into my kitchen between last night and this morning?

My mind went on wild tangents, ending up in a caffeine-deprived and improbable scenario. Bobby had just lost his front teeth, giving him an adorable, fanged smile and a lisp. Perhaps because my old machine had been on its last legs, the coffee fairy had left me a brand new one.

It made a hell of a lot more sense than someone breaking into my apartment last night, not to steal things, but to leave me new appliances.

No time for the mystery—I had to get Bobby to school. Still, I couldn't help glancing around on the way to Bobby's bedroom to wake him up, a sense of unease crawling up my spine. Someone had been here while we were sleeping—I certainly hadn't bought the machine or set it up on the counter. Nothing seemed out of the ordinary to my sleep-bleary gaze, but since our small apartment always looked like a toy tornado had come through, it was hard to judge.

I got Bobby breakfast and eyed the coffeemaker. My old, beat-up one was nowhere to be found in cupboards or under the sink, so if I wanted caffeine, I would have to use it. It took me two tries to figure out how to work the thing, and Bobby was chirping behind me about Animal Squiggles trading cards (the hot ticket item in elementary school this year) in between mouthfuls of his favorite sugary cereal, not noticing my struggle.

Two cups of coffee later, Bobby and I left the apartment. Despite pumping the pedals, my car made screeching noises instead of chugging to life, and so we ended up jogging the fifteen blocks to his school before I caught the bus to get to the far side of town.

My stop was five blocks from work, and the grey skies opened up just as I stepped out. A frantic scrabble in my purse yielded gum wrappers, but no umbrella. I tucked my bag under my hooded coat and ran for it.

The double doors swished open on the office building's shared lobby. The usual doorman, Jack, was absent. Sitting in his place behind the security console was a man I had never seen before.

He glanced up from the magazine he was reading. "Can I help you?" he asked as I paused in the lobby.

It was enough of a push to remind me about how late I was. "Sorry, just caught in the rain," I said, squelching my way towards the elevators. "I work here."

"Okay." He glanced back down.

In the elevator, I pressed the third-floor button. I don't know why people always look up and watch the floor numbers pass, even when alone—I did, too. When it dinged on my floor, I stepped out.

To nothing.

No, not literally nothing. There was an empty corridor leading to the door of the office. But the door was closed, the lights off. The magazine's logo—gone.

I walked up to the door. Tried the knob, which was locked. Peeked in through the window.

The desks and bookcases were empty, the ones that were left. Most had been removed, only one or two still littering the space. There was enough dust to indicate that it had been abandoned for at least several months, if not longer.

What the hell? I knew I hadn't gotten a lot of sleep, but there's no way this could have happened overnight.

Maybe the coffee machine fairy had made a second stop?

I walked downstairs this time, rather than taking the elevator, to give me time to think. I approached the man at the front desk. He glanced up, then back down to his magazine without acknowledging me.

"Hello," I said loudly. The security guard reluctantly lifted his eyes again. "What happened to the third floor?"

He shrugged, eyes scanning the ceiling as he rubbed his chin. "Used to be a magazine. They folded."

"When?"

He scratched his head. "Dunno. Before I was hired." He nodded at the mag he was reading. Instead of the *City Voice*, he held our competitor, the *Street Times*. "Last one in town."

I stared at it, then at him. My mind was blank. If the *City Voice* didn't exist anymore, then where did I work? My thoughts spun uselessly. "Where's Jack, the usual doorman?"

The man gave me a funny look. "Lady, I've been here for almost two years. Don't know any Jack."

"Oh." *Of course.* "Thank you."

I made my way outside where, thankfully, the rain had lessened. I was still soaking wet, but at least I could put up my hood as I stood under an overhang and tried to figure out my next move.

That's when I had a horrible thought and swiped open my cell to make a call. What if . . . ?

"Hello! Lincoln Elementary School."

"Hi! It's Susan Rose. I'm the mom of Bobby, who's in Mrs. Nichol's first grade class. Is he okay?"

There was an awkward paused, and I realized my calling out of the blue like this would seem a little strange. I filled in the silence by hedging, "He was feeling a little . . . he was coughing this morning. I just want to make sure he's not gotten sick."

"Oh, okay. Let me check. Can you hold?"

I fidgeted until the secretary came back on. "Mrs. Nichol says he seems fine, but she'll keep an eye on him."

Relief buzzed through me, and I sagged against the building wall. "Great, great. Thanks." I hung up.

For some reason, I'd had the terrible idea that since things were appearing and disappearing, Bobby would have gone "poof," too. The thought still niggled at the back of my mind—should I pull him from school, just in case?

But, honestly, he was probably better off there. There, he had his friends and teachers with him. Out here, I still didn't know what was going on. I wasn't going to risk him disappearing, too. Until I figured all this out, I needed him safe and accounted for.

Although, speaking of knowing people . . . I checked my cell. No one had texted or phoned. In fact, many of my usual numbers—Dave from the office, a friend from work, students whose writing I'd edited, Ed—they weren't in my list of contacts at all.

But there were a few new numbers in there. Who was "JJ?" And why did I have "Felicia's Dog Grooming Service" on my "recently contacted?"

It was a bit scary thinking of calling someone I didn't know at all, especially considering how this day had been going—someone whose name hadn't been in my phone yesterday. So I opted to call the dog groomers. Maybe we now had a pet, just like we had the new coffeemaker.

The phone picked up after seven rings, and the woman who answered spoke quickly, as if rushed. "This is Felicia. How can I help you?"

"Hi," I said. Then, for lack of a better option, "This is Susan Rose. May I ask—?"

"Susan!" the woman said sharply. "Where the hell are you?"

"I'm—" I glanced around. "I'm on the west side. I had a bit of car trouble."

Felicia blew out her breath with a sharp sound. "Why didn't you call? You know we're booked solid! Look, I try to put up with your schedule, but it seems like this always happens—"

"Wait," I interrupted. "What do you mean?"

"I'm sorry," the woman said. "I didn't want to do this over the phone, but I'm going to have to let you go. You can pick up your final check on Friday." The phone went dead.

Aha. Well, that answered the question of where I worked.

Or did. Did work, apparently. Since I'd just been fired.

I glanced at my contact list again. "JJ" stared back at me.

Well, the first phone call hadn't gone well. And my trip to work had been a bust. Maybe I should go home (if it was still there, which I was starting to doubt), regroup with another strong cup of coffee, and then try to figure out what was going on.

♦♦♦

Caffeine helped, especially since my key still worked and my apartment hadn't disappeared. At least, coffee helped me feel halfway human again after I changed out of my sodden clothes and got a warm cup in me.

I started to notice more differences in our home, small ones—new clothes in my closet when I was changing, some toy dinosaurs I'd never seen before, and a blue-striped duvet on my bed instead of the normal paisley one. But none of the changes cleared up any of this crazy situation. None of this made any sense, not unless I'd hallucinated the past number of years working at the magazine.

So . . . time to call that other number in my phone. The mysterious "JJ."

The phone rang and rang and rang. After a couple minutes, I got a generic voicemail message repeating the number I'd called in a monotonous voice and advising me to wait for the beep.

"Hi," I said when it started to record, and then paused. Hell, I probably should have rehearsed this part. I didn't think I would have a lot of time on voicemail to explain things . . . not that I had anything to explain, since I had no idea what was going on at all. "Um . . . it's Susan Rose. Can you please give me a call?"

I hung up. So now what? I glanced at the clock. It was nearly 11:30, so there was still a while to go until it was time to get Bobby from school.

Before I had gotten very far in my thoughts, my phone rang. "JJ" popped up on the screen, and I swiped the bar to open the call.

"This isn't great timing. What do you want, Susan?" the male voice said brusquely.

Taken aback, I said, "Look, I woke up this morning and everything was . . . different. Your number is in my phone, so I hoped you might know what's gone wrong."

There was a pause on the other end of the line. "What are you talking about?" The man's volume dropped and a worried note entered his voice. "Are you okay?"

I took a deep breath and explained a bit how my morning had gone. There was an even longer pause on JJ's end.

"What's really going on, Susan? Did something happen you're not telling me?"

I shook my head, even though he couldn't see it. "Look, I know it sounds nuts. *I* sound nuts, but I swear that things have changed overnight. All I can think is maybe I had some sort of head injury and I'm forgetting what's happened. But I feel fine, and that still doesn't explain why I would think I was working at the magazine yesterday, but it's closed today. Maybe the police could help?"

"Um, no. Don't involve the police." He hummed under his breath. "My lunch meeting was cancelled, so let's see if we can get to the bottom of this. Can you meet me at Eight Dragon Restaurant?" He gave me an address.

"Okay." The restaurant was located downtown by the history museum, where I'd taken Bobby for his birthday. "I can be there in twenty minutes."

The bus dropped me a block away from my destination. The restaurant was a hole-in-the-wall place with a steady stream of lunchers coming and going, mostly Chinese and mostly large groups. The conversations and shouting of waitresses and kitchen staff created an inferno of noise that bounced around the bare walls like a mass racquetball match. But the smells of the food were heavenly, and it made me realize I had skipped breakfast.

"How many?" barked the waitress/hostess over the din, and I told her I was meeting someone. "Sit now or wait?" she asked.

I thought I heard my name, then a hand gripped my elbow from behind. I spun around to face the man who had so casually touched my arm, to see someone completely unexpected.

I'd seen that face before. In fact, everyone in the city probably knew that face. "JJ" wasn't just anybody. "JJ" was Julian James, the former mayor. The one Ed had run an exposé on two years ago, which had led to Julian's suicide.

The room became hot and started to wobble around the edges. I pulled free of Julian's grasp and steadied myself against the waitress stand. This was impossible. There was no way that this could be real.

"You," I breathed faintly. "You . . ."

"Yes, me," he said with a wry twist of his mouth.

When James had first been elected, people said he was too young. He looked young still, even though his forty-odd years on this planet had produced thin lines around his mouth and eyes, plus a silvering at his temples. He was handsome, but too polished—his hair over-styled and gelled to solidity, his teeth too white. But the picture he tried to create wasn't perfect by any means. His smile was forced, and there was a hollowness behind his eyes that suggested he was haunted by something that was giving him restless nights.

"Table for two, please," he told the hostess, who nodded and squeezed us into a tiny space next to the banging doors of the kitchen. As soon as she was out of earshot, Julian said, "Is this just a trick to get me to talk to you again?"

Although a bit dazed, I had enough presence of mind to shake my head. "Seriously, I had no idea who you were when I called. Although I . . . I do now."

He smiled slightly, glancing down at the table. He fidgeted with his fork—nervously, I thought. "Why are you pulling this, Susan? I thought we'd agreed to wait."

"Look." I hesitated, but this all felt slightly unreal. "Um . . . first off, how do I know you? How did we meet?"

He gave me a look that flustered me. It was both worried and intimate to a degree that I hadn't experienced since Bobby's father, and the two of us had been barely out of our teens when I got pregnant and he left me on my own. Bobby's dad was the only man I'd ever been with. Though I couldn't imagine life without Bobby, I'd steered clear of relationships since then. I couldn't afford any more complications.

When I said nothing, trying to deny the look he'd given me, Julian casually scanned the restaurant as he belatedly answered my question. "We met at Felicity's Grooming when I took in Puddles—" at my blank look, he clarified, "—our dog. My wife's dog, actually. I didn't tell you I was married, at first. To be honest, I didn't want to."

"But I would *never*—" I protested, but stopped. I felt slightly sick. "Did I break it off with you when I found out the truth?"

Julian hesitated for a moment, then shook his head.

"Oh," I said. Almost to myself, I added, "I didn't think I would ever do something like that."

Julian patted my hand on the table, but didn't do more than that. "It was—well, my wife and I have been having a lot of problems. We married fresh out of high school and had our son when we weren't ready for the responsibility. We made it through, but we're different people now. We agreed to separate. However, break it off during an election year? It would kill me in the polls."

I opened my mouth to ask for more details, but realized I didn't want them. This other life—this other *me*—seemed miles different from where I'd started out. Instead of continuing on about an *us* I didn't remember and didn't want to remember, I began to talk. Details about my two lives came pouring out of me in a confused rush. I didn't know why I confessed everything, but it felt natural to talk to him. As if we'd known each other for years.

Working at the magazine. My son, and the intense fear he'd disappear just like my job had. The new possessions that had shown up in my apartment overnight. The exposé on Julian's fraud and embezzlement. Julian's suicide.

Through it all, he listened, with only a break to order food. When I came to the end, he said, "Hmmm." Nothing more for a moment.

I supposed I sounded crazy. *I* wouldn't have believed me. But, then again, I was talking to a dead man.

"I don't know what to tell you about the differences," he said. His mouth quirked. "But I do know one thing. There was no coffee fairy. I gave you that coffeemaker on our third date. After you told me you were allergic to flowers."

The unexpectedness of his statement made me laugh out loud. A bit hysterically, but it felt good to let out some tension. Julian just smiled, then the smile dropped from his face.

"As to something illegal going on—let's just say that someone might have known events were happening behind the scenes," Julian said. "Even if this person wasn't responsible for the crimes being committed, he wouldn't want the person responsible to get caught." He twisted his napkin on the table. "I always thought fighting for the right thing was black and white. That knowing about wrongdoing and taking action were tantamount to the same thing. But they aren't. Not when your own flesh and blood is involved. I can see that a man might take the fall in order to protect someone more important to him than his own life."

I raised my eyebrows. "So Ed made up his story? You weren't involved at all?"

Julian smiled, shrugging. He seemed much more relaxed than he did when we met at the restaurant's entrance. The haunted look was gone. "I've never committed fraud and embezzlement. I've certainly never murdered anyone. And this Ed character you keep mentioning? If he's a writer, it's not for the *Street Times*."

Something about what Julian said niggled at the edge of my consciousness. Something that had happened while I was editing Ed's follow-up article yesterday. Hadn't I said to myself that James *shouldn't* have committed the crimes? And here, today, he *hadn't* done it. And he was still alive.

The waitress approached once more and took Julian's credit card. After he paid, he leaned forward, but didn't touch me again. "I miss you," he said softly. It was hard to meet the intensity of his gaze, and I could feel the weight of our shared history in this other life. A life I knew nothing about, except that this man had been a large part of it. "But I need to win the election first—I'm doing a lot of good for this city. And then I need to figure out what to do about other elements. Repeating a tragedy like the one you mentioned—that wouldn't be in my best interests, now, would it?" Despite the joking tone, for a moment, he seemed tired and older. I wondered what I would do in his shoes.

However, there was one priority that I agreed about with him. If it came to Bobby or me, I would choose Bobby every time. No matter what it meant or whatever my son did.

"I don't know what's happening to you," Julian continued. "I wish I could help. One thing I do know—I would strongly advise against going to the police. It won't help you or Bobby, a strange story like this."

And not going to the police *would* help Julian, I couldn't help thinking cynically. Not confessing to the authorities what

I knew about *his* son's crimes. But, then again, I had no proof. And there was no reason for me to turn him in . . . right now.

I could see the same knowledge on his face, and that he knew I was able to pick up on his awareness. "I can't say I believe everything you've said. Honestly, it's a tough sell." I nodded in agreement. "But my suggestion would be to track down those people you believed you worked with at the magazine. If they're real people, then there must be a logical explanation. And they might be able to help you put together the events in your life much better than I could."

I nodded again, my mouth dry. From that glimpse of the connection between us, I could understand why I'd done what I'd done with Julian in this life (although it still bothered me that I'd abandoned my morals long enough to have an affair . . . and that I had an affair with such a handsome man and *couldn't remember a thing*), but it felt like his advice was on the right track.

"Thanks," I said. Then, because I could think of nothing else, "Good luck."

He nodded and left. It took me an extra minute before I collected my purse and headed back to the bus stop. I'd need to hustle to get to the elementary school for pick-up.

As soon as I saw Bobby, I lost the worst of the panicked confusion that had been riding my shoulders since that morning. I bent down to give him my usual hug, but held on a few moments longer, until he began to squirm. We walked home rather than take the bus, since the sun had finally come out. I asked him about his day, plus one or two leading questions—"Notice anything different today?" "Any new people at school?" —but he seemed unaffected by the change. Or he *was* affected—he was a part of this changed world, and I was the only outsider who knew about our other life. When I asked him about my new coffeemaker, for example, he told me that my friend had given it to me.

"What friend?"

"JJ," Bobby replied casually. "But he doesn't visit anymore."

I dropped the subject. I didn't want to know how big a part of our life "JJ" had been. Whatever involvement he'd had, it was too much.

After that, it was homework, playing, dinner, bed.

I'd just gotten back to the living room and was wondering where to begin searching for my old co-workers when my phone rang. I quickly swiped it open without noting the number, hoping the sound hadn't woken Bobby. "Hello?"

"Susan?"

Oh, my god. "Dave!" I practically shouted, then dropped my voice and paused, to see if there was any stirring from the next room. Nope—nothing. "Dave," I repeated in a whisper. "I am *so* glad to hear from you."

This time, the pause was on the other end. "You shouldn't be. I'm sorry, Susan. I couldn't do it anymore."

Dave's tone seemed ominous. "Do what?"

"I couldn't take the responsibility anymore. I've been doing it for years, and the stress . . . it became too much. I needed to take a break."

Lightbulb. "You're talking about changing our lives, aren't you?" I asked excitedly. "You know what's going on, don't you?"

Dave sighed. "Yes, I know. I know about all of it. I was in your shoes for many years, and it's a terrible place to be."

"So what's happening? How do I go back to the way things were?"

"The way things were?" Dave laughed, but the sound was rusty. "Why would you want to do that?"

I hadn't really had time to think about it. "Because . . . because, well . . ." I ran my hand through my long hair. "Because I don't like who I am here. Apparently, I've done things I shouldn't have."

"Haven't we all?" Without waiting for an answer, Dave continued. "We're safe here. It might be different, but you can't change the past. Not without Ed, and that's not going to happen."

"Why not?" I asked belligerently. "I want to go back."

"You can't," Dave repeated. "But this change will end it. Nothing else will shift, as long as you leave it alone. And that's what I'm warning you about—don't try. Just leave it alone." The phone beeped in my ear, and I realized he had hung up on me.

I frantically scrolled to my recent calls, and saw that the call had come from a blocked number. Damn.

I'd been a copy-editor for years. I knew how to fact-check, and I knew how to track things down. Dave said things wouldn't change without Ed. Well? First step: find Ed.

I sat down at my computer and opened a web browser.

Ed O'Hearne, Edward O'Hearne, Ed A. O'Hearne —I looked up all the variations of his name I could think of, but got zero hits for magazines. If he was a writer, he must be unpublished.

I scrolled to page two and three of the search. Okay… this might be something. A long-outdated Facebook page. No profile picture, but the age seemed right. I checked the posts, the most recent from a few years ago. He'd shared several pictures of what looked like younger versions of the Ed I knew (kids, maybe?), but no pics of himself. I followed through to the Facebook page of one of the older women in a picture, and hit paydirt.

It was his wife, and she was much more active online. Pictures, posts, little snippets of a life together. Lots of pictures of Ed and her.

They lived the next town over from me, so I friended her and sent a message asking if we could meet. That I'd found something of her husband's that he'd probably want back. I kept deliberately vague with the wording, trusting that based on her generally sweet-natured posts and the fact I was a woman living nearby that she would be more inclined to not question my flimsy excuse.

And she didn't. The next morning after I dropped off Bobby at school, she agreed to meet me for coffee. I chose Preston's Perk, a local coffee shop, usually busy and anonymous this time of the morning.

Ed's wife looked even sweeter in person, a grandmotherly type who'd have homemade cookies in a jar for the grandkids. We chatted about her children and my son for a few moments before I brought out my decoy—a dog-eared old biography from my college days. The cover was bright red, and I'd written Ed's name on the inside front cover. When I pointed out her husband's name to her, I told her I'd found the book in a magazine rack at the doctor's office and picked it up.

"That's strange," she said. Her fingers were swollen with arthritis, but she accepted the book and turned it over in her hands. "I don't remember this."

"Well, I figured it was important, since it had his name in it." I pointed again to the "evidence" I'd created, and she nodded. I added, "You can ask him about it when you give it to him."

I didn't understand why she didn't answer. Not until she fumbled in her purse and took out a tissue to wipe at her eyes did I realize she was crying. "I wish I could ask him." Her voice broke. "But he passed away a month ago. That's why I wanted so badly to know what you'd found . . ."

My heart sank. My plan had been to follow her back to her house, so I could talk to Ed. Although I hadn't liked the guy, I'd never expected this.

Dave had said Ed was the key to the change. Now, the rest of what Dave had said made sense. If Ed was dead, and he was the key, then I could do nothing.

But if that were the case, why had Dave been so set against me pursuing this? There must be something I was missing.

I realized the silence had gone on too long, and I belatedly replied, "I'm so sorry." I didn't know what else to say. Out of guilt, I sat with her for the next hour and listened to her ramble on about their life together . . . their kids and grandkids, Ed's job as an English teacher, his retirement three years ago, his sudden heart attack.

"Did he ever write stories at all?" I asked, more to make conversation than because I thought it would solve anything. I had been listening with half an ear for a while now.

"Oh, yes. He always wanted to be an author. He even wrote a book manuscript, but it was never published. One of his only regrets, I believe." Her eyes had dried up a while ago, but she now looked ready to cry again. "Why? Are you a writer, too?"

So *that's* why Dave warned me not to pursue any leads. Even though Ed was gone in this life, his writing was still around. It made me realize that that last day in my other life, it wasn't *Ed* I'd interacted with in person. It had been Dave. The only connection I'd had with Ed was through his story.

I had a sudden stroke of inspiration. "I'm an editor, actually," I said. "Tell you what? Why don't I take a look at his book, see if it has any promise? If you could get it published, it might be very fulfilling to your kids and grandkids to finally see his words in print. To realize a dream of his, even after his passing."

She sniffed, but nodded almost at once. "Oh, I would love that! I would be happy to have you look it over."

After exchanging contact information, I practically danced my way home. I waited breathlessly by my email, but I'd only been online for a few minutes before a new message dinged in my inbox. It was her.

I opened up the file and got to reading.

The thing that struck me right away was that the writing style was nothing similar to the article I'd edited before everything went haywire. This new Ed's style was precise and exact, but his composition was completely lifeless . . . almost as if I'd written it. On top of that, there wasn't a comma out of place, and the grammar was perfect. It had technique, but none of his usual flashy style.

The eerie part was the subject. It was about a mayor whose son had committed fraud and embezzlement, but he turned a blind eye to his son's crimes. The mayor was married, but having a heated affair with a pet shop owner. She was a short, curvy brunette who wore glasses.

A chill went through me, and I had to stop reading for a moment and take a few deep breaths. Finally, I nerved myself to scroll to the ending of the book.

It was both a relief and frustrating to see the manuscript stopped right in the middle of a sentence. I read back a few paragraphs. The last scene in the book took place late at night. The son was meeting an FBI agent down by the shipyards, supposedly to confess his father's crimes. Instead, he had a gun in his pocket and . . .

Calling up Ed's wife yielded some answers, at least about the book's style. Unlike "my" Ed, who'd schmoozed his way into a job and learned writing along the way, this one had gotten the full ride—college, honors, teaching. And some of what she was saying in particular stuck out.

"He was always correcting my grammar," she told me with a smile in her voice. "It was terribly annoying, but just who he was."

Good at editing, but bad at writing. From what I'd heard from his wife, he'd been a doting and selfless husband, and not at all the lying sleaze who would make up facts so his stories garnered widespread recognition. The total opposite of "my" Ed. I asked her when he had started being this way.

"Always," she told me. "I knew him since grade school, and he was terribly proper, even then. He knew exactly how to fix things—in fact, he helped tutor me in high school. That's how we became sweethearts."

I thanked her and hung up.

There was a connection between Ed's writing and the timeline change, that was obvious. But it wasn't *just* the writing that had changed things, I felt. There was a bond between Ed's writing and the editor who worked on it that made things different. As if somehow my editing his article had passed on that talent to him. And that skill had changed his direction in life. No longer was he fly-by-the-seat-of-his-pants, only-looking-out-for-himself Ed.

My phone began to ring, and when I glanced at the screen, it said "unknown number." I moved to swipe it to silence, but hesitated. After the fourth ring, right before voicemail, I tapped "speaker."

"Hello?"

"Susan?"

"Dave!" My tone was halfway between pissed and relieved. I went with belligerent. "Why are you calling again? I figured it out already." *Almost.* "There's nothing you can do to stop me."

"Look, I didn't want it to be this way." He sighed. "You have no idea what it's like. I'm exhausted, you know? You think you've got it fixed, you try to stick to the facts, but then something else changes, and suddenly the world's gone to shit. I couldn't take the pressure anymore."

Okay. Not exactly the explanation I was hoping for.

"So . . . ?"

"So everything's better this time. No more Ed means no more stories. No more competing timelines. No more places where good intentions can lead us astray. We'll live our lives in peace."

"But I can't," I argued. "In this life, I have no job. I've abandoned my morals. I don't want to live like this. I want to be a good role model for my son, not . . . this person." For a few moments, all I heard from the line was heavy breathing. I raised my voice. "I'm going to do this whether you help me or not, Dave. So if you don't want things to go to badly . . ."

He sighed. "It's not a science, you know. And if you take us back to our old timeline, I won't interfere. But if the world ends in nuclear warfare, that's on your head, not mine."

I took a deep breath. "Things can change that much?"

"Yeah." He snorted. "He's a wild card, and the power is tied up in him. But the control is in you. You have to rein in his words. It's the only way to keep everything safe."

"Fine. Okay, tell me what I need to do."

♦♦♦

I picked up Bobby from school and the rest of the day seemed normal, at least from an outside perspective. Hopefully to Bobby, especially. But to me, time was ticking by like an ant crawling across the Grand Canyon. By the time I finally put Bobby to bed and gave him our twenty kisses, I thought my stomach would explode with anxiety.

Time to tackle this monster manuscript. There was no time to be subtle. As best as I could recall, I rewrote Ed's original article about James' suicide and the interview with James' son, cutting out huge swathes of Ed's technically polished chapters. I made typos, missed commas, and added run-on sentences galore. "James is guilty as hell," I whispered over the article, feeling silly to be talking to the words on the screen. "Put everything back the way it was." And then I saved the book file and pulled out my sleeper sofa.

As soon as my alarm went off in the morning, I scrabbled for my cell and flipped immediately to my contacts.

Dave, Ed, friends from work—they were all back in place. No Felicia's Dog Grooming Service. And no JJ.

It had worked. It had actually worked. Things were normal again, as far as I could tell. But that made me curious—there was just one more thing I felt I needed to check.

I opened a webpage and typed in "Julian James."

"—committed suicide," I read aloud.

Damn. I knew that putting the world back the way it had been would also put James back into the role of the corrupt and suicidal politician. But after having seen the other side of him—the personal side, the side who would do anything to prevent his son from taking a fall—it was hard not to think about what I had done by adjusting the timeline exactly back the way it had been. Hard not to wonder if it was the right thing. Also hard not to wonder if I had the power to change the timeline into something better.

Especially since the new and improved Ed, who had turned out to be a decent person and shared a life with a wonderful woman, was gone again. In his place would be the lying sleaze who couldn't remember my name.

Here, I had work and could take care of my son. Here, I had my morals intact.

There, a good man who loved his son was still alive. Still working on helping the city, even if he made some mistakes along the way.

I popped some aspirin to deal with the headache these thoughts created, and got Bobby off to school. Then I went to work—a work that was, thank goodness, there again. I was back to the grind, back to a steady paycheck, back to a car that worked, albeit grudgingly.

Near the end of my shift, Dave shuffled by and dropped a stack of typewritten pages on my desk. "Remember, I won't help again," he muttered to me. "Don't mess this up." He shuffled off.

I gingerly picked up the pages and started to read.

Unlike the article from a few days ago, this was a feel-good piece. A prominent couple celebrating their fiftieth year of marriage. The husband was a world-renowned poet, the wife a retired actress.

In some small way, the couple reminded me of the life the other Ed had had. In this life, he'd never been married, never had kids.

I picked up my red pen to edit the story, but put it down again.

I could edit the article and try to keep this reality intact. Or I could try to change the facts and change reality into something better.

But if I did that, would we instead go back to that other life? The one where Ed was dead, but had lived a long and happy life in the meantime—a better person, who had destroyed no one else's life in the process? The one where Julian was alive to fix the wrongs his family had done, rather than be the fall guy for terrible crimes he didn't commit? The one where I had given up some part of myself in order to love someone other than Bobby?

And who was I to make that choice? What if I messed it all up, like Dave said? I was supposed to be the one in control—the one who kept things steady. Knowingly trying to change other peoples' lives . . . that seemed egotistical, and wrong.

I thought of Bobby who I would do anything for, and I thought of Julian—trying to save the city and destroying his own life in the process. The other Ed, a good man with a family who loved him.

There was no one to help me if I failed. So should I even try?

I bit my lip. I sighed.

And I picked up my pen again.

♦ ♦ ♦ SIREN SONG ♦ ♦ ♦

RAIDNE RAN THE TALONS OF her long-fingered feet through Teles's sea-green hair and crowned it with an ivory comb. Shaped like birds, but with the faces and torsos of women, the sirens were dexterous with their claws in the absence of human hands.

"Descant," her sister told Teles gently, and the two sirens sang together until their older sister Molpe pushed her way between them. She shook the feathers of her wings in their faces.

"No, no, don't teach the baby the low notes," Molpe said, but not cruelly. She was smiling as she spoke. They were family, and family protected one another.

Even so, Teles burned at the casual word her sister threw at her. "I'm no baby," she said fiercely, but Molpe just laughed at her and wandered back towards the beach. The sea was in the sirens' blood; it was hard for any of them to be away from it too long.

"Be patient." Raidne caressed her hair. "There will be a time for you soon. Don't forget what I have taught you."

It was hard for Teles to wait, since she was left alone each day as her sisters did their important work. Only the singing of her siblings kept her company as the sun god Sol rode through the sky, the living music of the sirens' voices carried inland to her with the breeze.

Raidne was closest to Teles in age, and often took sympathy on her. Once in a while, her sister would bring back souvenirs from the shipwrecks the sirens caused. The sirens would use their hypnotic voices to lure sailors close to shore, where the humans' boats would crash open on the jagged teeth of rocks protecting the bay. Last time, Raidne had brought her little sister the delicate comb now gracing Teles's hair.

"I pulled it from a land-woman's head," she told her. "Her hair was brown as mud, but her eyes were green, like the waters running through your hair. So I knew it was meant for you."

From her perch on the immovable land, Teles heard the song of her sisters push out over the ocean like a net awaiting a catch. With all her heart, she wanted to be with them, be a part of them. Only a few more years, and they would let her. When she took her maiden flight, she would be able to claim her place at their side. She fell asleep in the dappled light under the trees, listening to her sisters sing.

And woke, aware of something terribly wrong.

She awoke to silence.

Teles lifted her head. The sea hissed up the sand of the beach and the gulls cried as they sliced through the sky, but the voices, ever-present for as long as she could remember, were gone. Their song had ended and no new song begun.

She stood on her spindly bird legs and crept out from the shade of the woods. The sun was westering over the sea and its light had turned scarlet. The beach was empty, and her feathers ruffled from the breeze off the ocean.

When she reached the circle of rocks where the sisters lured sailors with their song, she croaked out their twelve names, starting with the eldest and ending with her favorite sisters, just a few decades older than her. Molpe. Raidne.

No one answered. There was no one to answer. The rocks were bare.

The small island seemed impossibly large without her sisters there. Teles wandered around it as the sun sank over the waters. She finally returned to the treacherous rocks of the natural harbor where the sirens spent their days.

Pillowing her head on her wings, she wept. Only the sea was there to shush her tears, and it was a cold and heartless comfort that it gave her.

♦♦♦

The sky brightened over the sand and Teles woke slowly. There were no dreams remembered, and she was surprised at the fear she felt as she lay drowsing--until the discordant calls of the gulls reminded her of a lack.

Music was missing. Her sisters were missing.

The quiet was unbearable. Thinking of Molpe, thinking of Raidne, her voice trembled as she sang hesitantly to the ocean waters, missing more notes than she struck. When her throat dried up and the sun was fierce overhead, she closed her mouth and retreated to the copse of trees in the center of the island to rest. When the sun headed west, she wandered the circuit of the beach, calling name after name, unanswered.

Why would they disappear? What could have happened to them that they would leave her behind?

The next day, the sea was grey, the skies stirred up by the gods. Something fierce was coming, and she had no one to protect her from it. On god-called storms, the sisters would retreat to the shelter of their trees and huddle together until the violence passed.

Almost in defiance of the coming tempest, Teles sang from the lee of the harbor for comfort until the waves and the winds pushed her inland.

She found the sirens' old nest in the center of the trees, a bramble of deadfall and feathers, long green hair, and bits and pieces of dead mens' clothes. A home built for thirteen, she rattled around it like a pebble in a cup as the winds blew and the rains came down. Finally, she burrowed as far under the edges of it as she could and covered her body with her wings. The winds pulled at her and Zeus threw thunderbolts over the ocean.

Water poured from the skies, and she was drowning, over and over, until the drops slackened. An endless time later, the rain sizzled and faded into a mist. Teles stood, shaking out her wings as the storm passed away to the east.

Without thinking, she began to beat harder and faster with her wings, channeling her breathing into short huffs as she struggled. Crouching down, she gave an almighty push with her legs and leapt up, fiercely pounding at the clean air. Her wings caught at the mist, tearing it to shreds as she rose above the treetops under her own power and flew up, up, up into the air above the nest.

In the storm's wake, the sun glared down in a glory of reds and oranges as it descended into the west. The air was new, and she opened her mouth and sang, shaking her feathers and altering her bearing. With scooping motions back and forth with her limbs, she reversed her momentum and landed heavily in the waterlogged sands of the beach, staggering clumsily and dropping to her knees. She continued to sing, a melody of joy at her first flight, a cascade of notes rising up into the sky.

It was so beautiful that the thunder god paused in his far-off journey, paused to listen to the last siren sing. Until the rains lashed at him again, the business at hand calling Zeus's attention back to his job, and he turned away, distracted.

Having felt the sky god's attention, Teles remembered her sisters, even in the midst of her joy. Her song changed, became the dirge sung at sunset, a farewell to Sol, the sun god.

The notes sank into the waters, and she turned towards the harbor only to notice something she had never seen before. Among the rocks, a shape: a boat, jagged with torn sails, but miraculously whole in the waters. It was small enough that it had avoided the rocks so deadly to larger ships. Standing on its deck, a single man. His eyes were trained on her as she sang, but they were wide open and unseeing, caught in her hypnotic voice.

Raidne had shown them to her before, these horrible land-people, but only after they were safely drowned. Teles had never seen a live one.

"We sing because we must," Raidne had told her younger sister at the time, kissing her cheeks and making her giggle.

"We will let no man be our master. Pluto will call us to die before that happens."

The man had black hair, wet from the rains. His eyes were grey, but a color so vivid that they seemed uncontainable, like the storm just passed. She saw that he breathed, his chest rising and falling as he stood there, and she altered her voice. *Come here*, said her song.

His body moved at her command, stepping over the edge of the small boat and dropping to the sandy floor of the sea. The waters reached his waist, and he came crashing through their roughness until he splashed up onto the shore. *Stop*, said her song, and he halted before her.

Teles closed her mouth, the notes stilled on her tongue. The man's liquid eyes stared down at her, uncomprehending and blank. She had never seen a live human before. Curious, she reached up and dared to put the tip of her wing against his face.

There was a sound like a sea gull's cry, then sudden movement. She found herself pushed down, landing in an ungainly heap on the sand. Blinded, she coughed at the sand kicked into her face, scrabbling at her eyes with her wings. It was an instinctual reaction, but useless. Her eyes were powerless, even if they were open.

A blade descended, a shaft of vengeance, a shining silver and mortal instrument, and it tore through her breast and pinned her to the ground. As her blood fell into the sand, she saw the melting grey of the man's eyes staring at her, and she realized the truth too late. Too late, she knew why her sisters had hated. Too late, she knew what had happened to them while she had been sleeping that day.

Death before mastery. She, their one hope, had been left behind.

She, too, had failed.

Teles opened her mouth to sing a retaliation, but her tongue was stoppered with the taste of iron, and her lungs staggered as she tried to breathe. The man splashed back to his boat, sheathing his bloody sword as he walked. Mute, she watched as he reclaimed the oars in the bottom of his ship and rowed away. He did not look back.

Her breath bubbled in her throat. The distant rumble of fading thunder drummed across the horizon as the sun fell in bloody ribbons into the cold ocean waters. The clouds streamed out across the glory of the storm-kissed sky, and the gulls cried mournfully as they flew away.

♦ ♦ ♦ THE RACE ♦ ♦ ♦

MELINDA PLUNGED INTO THE OCEAN, but Paul quickly pulled ahead of her using steady strokes. She really shouldn't have boasted in front of everyone that she was the better swimmer, pricking Paul's ego.

Her friends chanted her name from the shore, encouraging her. Even with lungs burning and muscles aching, she put on a burst of speed at the sound. It wasn't quite enough to make a difference. When the sea monster rose up out of the depths, Paul was still far in the lead.

Darn. He had been a good boyfriend, too.

At least she won the race.

♦ ♦ ♦ IN MOURNING ♦ ♦ ♦

GEORGIA'S EYES WERE MILKY WITH cataracts, blind. A navy suit hung in the closet of the room, long-skirted and somber for the occasion. Not black—*too formal*, she'd thought when in the store a few months back. Navy conveyed regret without being in-your-face about all this funeral business. And the color of the suit matched her once-clear eyes. "Blue as the coming twilight," her husband told her when they'd first met.

Arthur had been young then and filled with the poetry of youth. So had she, never knowing the waste of years ahead—not *wasted* years, mind, but time had a way of wasting itself, of being taken advantage of and discarded like yesterday's candy. Thrown away, piece by piece, until the sweetness was gone and the outer wrapping was finally discarded, too.

Dressed, she looked more herself. Or what she'd always thought of herself, even with all the hard years stacked up behind her. Those early days of the marriage, before the kids had come—oh, how they'd enjoyed themselves! Dancing every Saturday night, regular as clocks. No worries of leaking pipes or snotty noses—no headaches, raised voices, slammed doors. Just laughter and music every weekend.

She looked too stiff when finally dressed, her joints gnarled and bent with age. Not how she'd pictured she'd look in her beautiful suit. Her thinning white hair was brushed away from the spotted skin of her forehead and hairsprayed into her usual half-foot coif. It was the way proper ladies used to wear their hair.

Not like now, not with these girls growing up today. Forget about the kids her grandchildren's age. Some of them shaved their heads like men. They had boyish bodies too, thin and sticklike with no breasts or hips. No *curves*. Short hair was fine, but it needed a certain tilt to it. A feminine woman made a man feel like a man. Girls today—was it any wonder there was so much divorce?

Not Arthur and her—no question that they'd lasted. They'd lasted forever. 'Til death do us part.

Collar adjusted just a tad, but it didn't seem to make much of a difference. She supposed it didn't matter how she looked. That wasn't the point of the funeral, was it? The point was remembering the life of the deceased—celebrating it, in fact. Not worrying about how one old lady looked in a suit.

She was ready—but these things always ran slow. Georgia had to wait.

Was her ride even here yet? She hadn't driven a car since her eyes grew dim and her hands lost their steadiness. It made more sense to stop driving rather than let them take away her license—so it became her choice, not theirs. Though it was frustrating, always being dependent on others. Arthur had driven for years longer than she did, but he was crazy stubborn. Always had been.

She'd hated that about him.

But during the illness, he'd smiled every time he saw her, smiled as if he were looking at her fifty years ago for the first time—despite the deterioration, despite the pain he felt.

Stubborn old cuss. She'd loved that about him.

The clock ticked. Where were they?

Finally, footsteps sounded outside. Finally, the door opened.

Time to go.

♦♦♦

Arthur was the first one in the room. He moved through the space in a slow shuffle, but he eventually reached her side, gently touched her face. His palm was warm and solid and familiar.

He moved his hand upwards to close the mahogany lid. Darkness followed light.

She had seen him, and there was no reason any reason to linger. She had said her goodbyes, long before this moment.

Georgia stretched and eased past Arthur standing beside her, head bowed. She felt a magnetic pull that grew stronger as she drifted into the air. Six men picked up the coffin and carried it towards the door, but she no longer felt tethered to it. Arthur shuffled after.

Her eyes turned back before the sky closed over her head. She would take with her one last glimpse, one last moment, one last memory.

Now, she could finally fly free.

♦ ♦ ♦ THE LAST BATTLE ♦ ♦ ♦

WHEN RIKIKO WAS YOUNG, HER father put her on top of a horse and handed her a naginata—a wickedly curved blade topping a long pole—three times as long as she was tall. Her arm trembled with the strain of holding it out from her side just as he showed her.

"You will be a great warrior," he told her as he adjusted her elbow slightly to give her more balance. "And the name of Koizumi will echo through the centuries."

He didn't smile at her. He seldom did—although she noticed that the corners of his eyes crinkled as he noticed her strong grip. His own version of a smile, which was a rare sign of approval from him.

So, "Yes, Father," she said, and kept her arm steady. He spent the rest of the day with her, leaving only at nighttime to take himself off to his own affairs, depositing her back to her rooms and her many hovering attendants.

"I shall watch your progress," he promised before he left.

The next morning, her maid dressed her in a brown tunic and pants instead of her usual ladies' robe. *Another day spent with Father.* Her heart jumped. The unexpected material of her new clothes swished around her legs and distracted her as she walked out the door, so she did not at first notice the white-haired man waiting for her in the shadowy hallway. In fact, she probably would have walked right by him unless he hadn't stepped directly into her path and made his bow.

When he stood up from his obeisance, she saw that his face was crisscrossed by scars, a web of white against his dark skin. The scars looked as if they had been made in deliberate patterns, almost like an elegant character written by a master calligrapher's hand. His left arm was twisted into a hard and unnatural angle held tightly against his chest, but his right arm was limber and corded with muscle.

"The lord has sent me," he told her. "Your training begins today."

She bowed in return and masked her disappointment behind her downturned eyes. "Yes, Master," she said.

He told her his name was Akihiro. She asked if he was related to the legendary Akihiro who had died in battle against the Khan's invasion of Japan a decade before she was born. Master Akihiro's eyes didn't flicker, but there was a long silence after her question. Finally, "Yes," he said, and no more.

The initial lesson began with the eight disciplines of body and breath. She mastered the first two within a matter of weeks—one was just sitting still for long hours at a time in focused meditation. Although she was supposed to be ruminating about war games, she often found her mind wandering far from the new things she was learning about stroke, counterstroke, balance, and breath.

Instead, she dreamed about Amaterasu, the sun goddess—beautiful and beloved by all. The world existed solely for the her benefit, much as Rikiko felt the household followed the sun of her younger sister, the beautiful and beloved Miwa.

Sometimes, Rikiko wished she was named for the goddess rather than burdened with a family name meaning strength. What girl wanted to be strong? Strong, maybe, to bear children. Strength of character, perhaps. But strength by itself, without any counterpart, seemed flawed and lonely.

Her father came to her after six months had passed. She had seen him distantly, but he had not again spent an entire day with her. Now, he watched from the side of the training ground as she swung her naginata, meeting each stroke of the Master with the correct counterstroke. She was tempted to glance over, which gave the Master opportunity to send her sprawling onto her back when she missed her parry. She caught her breath and glanced up, but her father was already gone.

The disciplines grew more complex. The winter rains yielded to blossoms and the temperate heat of summer, and then returned to rain. She was outfitted for makeshift armor on her twelfth birthday, and the next year outfitted again when her growing wrists poked out from the old sleeves. Under the supervision of her master, she spent long hours training next to the seasoned warriors, who affectionately called her *chiisana ohimesama*, or "little princess."

At the seventh discipline, she stalled. No matter what coaching Master Akihiro gave her, she couldn't move her mind away from her upcoming sixteenth birthday. If her mother had been alive, perhaps Rikiko would have been promised in marriage or even anticipating her first child. Instead, her little sister Miwa had married the son of the neighboring Tachibana clan. He was a year older than Rikiko, and he had the kindest smile she had ever seen. But he had married her golden sister, who was beloved and beautiful. Two things Rikiko would never be.

Rikiko only had a sprained ankle to show for her thoughts about this. Rather than paying attention to the road she traveled on when returning from her sister's wedding, she fell when her horse shied at a hare leaping across the path.

Bad timing for her. And a bad omen for the Koizumi.

Her father had just returned from a meeting with the Tachibana as they upheld their nomination for the throne against Mizumoto's claim. The Mizumoto had sprung a surprise candidate from the Watanabe clan in the conference of noble families, and backed their candidate with a less-than-idle threat. Troops were already gathering, and under normal circumstances, she would be riding with her father to meet them, now that her sister's wedding was finished.

"My steward will run the estate while I am gone," he told her severely. Her punishment, since she was her father's heir and trained to act in his stead. She bowed her head beneath his disapproval. "You, I expect to see recovered when I return."

Days passed, and news trickled to them that the first meeting had become a tense standoff. Each day, Rikiko waited to hear the news the standoff had broken into either battle or peace. Yet the bonds of her injury were her own fault, and so she could do nothing but gingerly climb to the top of the tower ladder to watch and hope for word.

♦♦♦

Two weeks into the standoff, from atop her daily vantage point, Rikiko watched a boy limping towards the gates. Behind him, a trail of bloody footprints stretched down the road in mute testimony to the urgency of his message. She came down from the tower to meet him, having recognized from his features that he was the son of a distant cousin.

"I have ridden day and night," he told her, eyes downcast, "until my horse collapsed in exhaustion. I left him there, and have run since."

"When was this?"

"A day ago. Maybe more, I don't know." He shook his head, too tired to focus. Master Akihiro was behind her, his mouth pinched into a thin line.

"Your news, cousin?" she prodded gently when it appeared the boy would fall. He was so pale, he looked like a ghost. To carry this message to her, he had worn through his shoes on the rocky terrain and continued despite the pain.

With his eyes trembling on the floor and his voice trembling in his throat, he recounted how he had been on the battlefield and seen the death of her father. An arrow struck the lord from his horse, and he had been trampled in the thick of battle.

Through the shock of hearing the news, she gave the boy her thanks and allowed him to be led away from the meeting in order to rest and heal. She ordered her best physicians to tend him.

Despite her desire to set out at once by herself to avenge her father, she instead took a deep breath and summoned the steward to inform him of the news.

As the last words left her lips, the steward sank to his knees in dramatic grief and began sobbing. It steadied her when she saw the older man's obvious sorrow, even if she knew her own face was white from shock and her lips hurt from biting them. But she had not cried a single tear.

"What do we do?" he whispered. From his tone, he was not really asking her.

"You will inform the captains. We march at once for the shogunate."

"No, there is too much to do. We must send word out to the—"

Her voice cut across his like a knife. "I did not realize you were now lord of this clan. I did not realize you carried the name Koizumi," she said bluntly.

He stared up at her. She saw his lashes flicker.

"At once, my lady," he finally said. He didn't bother to wipe away his tears as he stood up, bowed, and left the room.

By this time, the armies knew her, the odd daughter of the lord who spent her days training by their side. When she limped to face them and spoke about marching with the dawn, she was unsurprised to hear a low wave of muttering. She expected to hear them speaking down to her, like the steward had. She expected them to call her "little princess." But it still took her by surprise when one of the soldiers, someone she had known her whole life, stepped up and shouted at her, "Go back to your nursery, little girl." A chorus of agreement rang out, but not so much as she had feared.

Rikiko looked to her captains. They looked back.

The decision was hers. She nodded at her senior captain. He passed the nod onto his two junior captains, who approached the heckler. With her training master a comforting presence at her back, she watched as the soldier was held steady, stripped to the skin, and a whip applied until blood ran. When they finally released the man's arms, he fell to the ground with a thud, having passed out during the punishment and not able to bring up his arms to catch himself.

When she asked if there were any more objections, the other men held still. After that, the armies marched with her in the morning.

She, herself, did not sleep a single hour that night. Every time she closed her eyes, she saw one of her men bringing down the bloody whip across the skin of a soldier she had once known and respected. A man who would follow her no longer.

As the troops strung out in loose rows behind her on that first day, the temptation to look back was nearly overwhelming. After the previous day's incident, she wondered if the faces she saw would be friendly or hostile. Perhaps they would just be neutral. The back of her neck itched with the weight of eyes, but she continued to bite her lip instead of giving in to the temptation to turn. Her mouth was definitely turning black and blue from this new abuse she had devised for herself. In spite of everything, the thought made her smile.

On the second day, a shout went up on their left flank. News quickly passed through the troops—riders approaching. Rikiko fumbled with her naginata as she unstrapped it from the side of her saddle, and it felt odd in her hand, suddenly unfamiliar. Although she adjusted her grip, her fingers were still sweaty with nerves and she wondered if now battle was approaching, she would drop the blade without a blow struck.

It wasn't until she saw the contingent of men in colorful armor riding up to her that she recognized them. Well, she recognized her sister's husband instantly, but the others she guessed, based on their position and armor. They did not remove their helmets when they rode up, and the distance between them made their faces new and strange under the helms, cast with odd and threatening shadows. She wondered what they saw when they looked at her, a woman dressed up as a man and awkwardly holding a naginata in threat. She quickly put away her weapon and bowed low in the saddle. They returned the gesture.

Camp was made early, since the group brought news of troop movements. She filled her belly with the plentiful vegetables, *umeboshi,* and rice cooked over the open fires, but didn't open her mouth except to eat. The meeting went long into the night, and she had to stifle yawn after yawn as the men argued over her head.

Her naginata gleamed in the virgin light of the lamps, a reminder that the men who argued so fiercely were years her senior. They had fought in what was being called the Battle of Mizumoto, the one where her father had been killed. She might as well have been married at the time instead of her sister, for all the good she had done for her clan. Her spirits sank the longer the meeting went on, until the clan heads finally said their farewells. Nothing had really been settled, and she returned to her tent for a few hours of snatched sleep while the sun rose over the hills. It was decided they would reconvene at noon.

After the second meeting, when the voices died down in the early hours of the afternoon, she demurely agreed with their plans when asked by Tachibana. She would march east with the main force, and they would split into their separate clans at the mountains. It was hard to anticipate what the Mizumoto would do—if their armies would meet them there for another engagement or if they would circle around to the exposed land at their backs. No one could agree on tactics. The Mizumoto had a new general, a second son who had the hot temper and cool soul of a dragon. They had not anticipated that first battle with him as their enemy—and they had lost. No telling what would happen in the coming fights.

After that, the days on the road stretched to weeks. They fought a series of surprise and pitched engagements, and her naginata was no longer unbloodied after the first attack. The confusion and dust of the fight concealed its more gruesome horrors from her, but she never forgot that first battle. Although, as time passed, the series of fights began to blur together with their very sameness. She lost her appetite as the weeks wore on and death marched at their side, only forcing herself to eat each night. When they camped one evening by a lake, Rikiko was surprised at the face that looked back at her from the calm surface of its waters. Her features were drawn with fatigue and her cheeks thin as a boy's. Lines had appeared around her nose, her mouth. A permanent check of worry was etched between her brows.

The weeks blurred together as the seasons turned and became months and more months, the roads stretching out to infinity. Right before the end of the second year, a soldier managed to give her three slashes across her face before she killed him. The slashes became infected and she spent days being nursed back to health, feverish and hallucinating about men long dead. Her father came to her in her fever dreams and spoke to her about the importance of family honor and vengeance. "I'm trying," she told him, again and again. But in every single dream, he turned his back on her and walked away as she cried out for him to return.

Although the hallucinations faded when she recovered, leaving only a lingering feeling of disappointment, the marks from the dead man's blade did not disappear. The white scars cut across her sun-browned cheeks, giving the appearance of the written character *omo*, meaning *lord*. The nickname stuck among her troops, and she became known far and wide as Koizumi Omo.

As the years of war passed, Koizumi Omo's blade dripped with the lifeblood of her enemies. Sometimes she saw in the eyes of the men she commanded that they'd forgotten she'd ever begun life as a woman. The bitter curse of her scarred face was recognized, respected, revered, feared. Everything her father had predicted had come to pass. Her name echoed, and the echoes were bloody.

At the end of countless inconclusive battles, she received a direct missive from her sister's husband, his bold pen strokes so familiar to her. The Tachibana were trapped at their castle by treachery from within. She must ride at once to rescue them.

She should have known better, but the note had been from *him*. So the trap laid in wait was sprung, and the reinforcements she commanded rode straight into the enemy's ambush.

She fought, and the heads of her enemies flew through the air, but each word she muttered under her breath was a curse against herself. She could feel the sun goddess Amaterasu overhead pricking at her conscience as her troops held their ground against the larger force, could feel each heartbeat as a second of delay became a minute . . . became an hour. Her blade rose and fell, and the hours fell to the ground with it.

Later, she was told that they had to wrestle her from her horse after they had disarmed her. They covered her so deeply in chains that she could only walk with the smallest of steps, and still she fought on. While she continued trying to fight for freedom, her sister's clan was wiped out in the East, every man, woman, and child falling to hostile blades. Her golden and beloved sister was killed, too—and her sister's husband.

It had seemed a needless precaution the week before, but Rikiko thanked Miwa's caution with every rattle of the cart which transported her to the capital to receive punishment. At Miwa's urging, Rikiko's nephew had been moved in secret to castle Koizumi barely a week before the fall of the Tachibana clan. He was safe in her cousin's household, and he had been given the new name of Koizumi.

He was all that she had left of clan Tachibana. The only link to what might have been.

The chains were struck only after she was brought before the chief advisor of the Watanabe clan. Of course, it was a Mizumoto, the same son of the clan who had killed her father. But, really, she had no choice. She signed the pact when it was brought before her, sealing it with the marriage of a distant cousin of hers to a younger son of theirs. She signed it, and she was set free. The head of the Watanabe clan, supported by the Mizumoto, became shogun in an intricate ceremony that she wasn't invited to, and the civil war ended with one stroke of the pen.

The war had aged her. In five years, she had learned the skills it took to run a clan the size of Koizumi. She'd learned delegation and how to mete out punishments. She'd learned how to fight and kill a man with no regrets.

But most of all, she'd learned sorrow. When the war ended, she looked back on the girl she had been before the war, and she felt as if that girl were a ghost.

All these lessons haunted her, but she held onto them with both hands, lest she forget what had started the war. The years passed, and she taught all that she had learned to her nephew, just as Master Akihiro had taught her. As peace and forgetfulness flowed by and covered up the ashes of the past, she held on.

On her nephew's sixteenth birthday, a little over a decade after the fall of the Tachibana, she called her nephew into the great hall. Seated on either side of her were two men several years younger than her. She saw at once that her nephew understood why they were there, schooled as he was in over a decade of her bitterness.

"May I present to you my heir, Koizumi Satoshi. This is Haru and Hinata of the Ito clan." Rikiko studied her young nephew waiting in front of her—a grown man, but still so young, his eyes untroubled. He looked so much like his father that it would once have made her heart hurt, but she no longer felt the pain. She felt nothing now. "Nephew," she said, and he bowed his head to her obediently. "We begin the long journey to avenge your parents. In a week's time, we march on the shogunate."

"Yes, Aunt," he said.

Once, her heart would have broken at his calm and accepting words. But her heart had broken long ago, before he was even born.

♦♦♦

The armies gathered in the open plains before the mountains. They would travel along the river valley, which led directly to the seat of the Watanabe shogunate. As they traveled, they would absorb the smaller clans into their armies, those who had already pledged to their cause.

Rikiko had had many years to plan her revenge. Years—and patience learned. Her nephew rode behind her; the two brothers of the Ito clan rode at her side. Being younger than her, they had not fought in the earlier wars, and so it had been agreed in advance that she would lead their combined forces.

As they rode, she remembered her first journey through this river valley as a new and untrained warrior. Also, she remembered her last—her failure to save Tachibana.

The weather was warm for spring, and the burgeoning life in the countryside called to her spirits. Camp was easy each night, and they made good speed. They met no opposition as the hours passed, but Rikiko had no illusions they were not anticipated. The dust of passage alone was enough to send up a cloud behind them, like a flag into the sky. They traveled with this shadow behind them, and she tried not to think of it as some message from the gods. It was natural, and nature traveled as a companion with them every day of their journey. The weather was beautiful, the sun fierce, and it made her think again of Amaterasu after all these years, the goddess who rose above all others. One legend in particular about the sun goddess spoke about when she fought against her brother and nearly destroyed the world. Because she was so important, her brother had been cast from Heaven in order to appease her. Rikiko couldn't help but start to think about the many failings of siblings, but stopped her thoughts before they went any further down that dark path.

On the fifth day, Rikiko was not the only one to see an answering cloud of dust rising in the sky before them. "A day out," estimated Haru at her side.

"Good defense, that old castle, there," said Hinata, pointing.

Rikiko glanced at her nephew at the sight of the structure, but his face was blank. Either he didn't recognize the castle, or he was a more suave diplomat than she had taken him for.

"A better position," she finally agreed. They turned their path slightly, so they rode into the rising sun and through the crumbling gates of the abandoned castle Tachibana. Here, her nephew had been born. Here, her sister had died in the last battle that ended the great war.

For the remainder of that day, she organized archers along the perimeters of the walls. By nightfall, they could see the campfires of the army surrounding them. The enemy was larger by far than their own force, and they attacked with the rising sun.

For several handfuls of days, Rikiko held them off with the strength of her will alone. Her armies looked up to her, the woman with the scarred face, leading every charge from the castle's gates, single-handedly turning back entire sections with the strength of her arm. Blades could not touch her. She seemed to have a protective circle around her—every night, she returned to the castle weary, but unwounded. Even her nephew took cuts at the vulnerable junctures of his armor, although never a serious wound.

It could have been the nineteenth day, or perhaps the twentieth, when they saw from their towers an approaching force. It was small, but the banners they carried were clear: it was the shogun.

♦♦♦

"This is it," Rikiko told her warriors as the sun rose the next morning. "He is here, finally. The coward could not remain hidden forever. Today, we will end this."

She mounted, and the men looked to her, followed as if compelled by a force greater than themselves. As she spun her naginata with ease, her eyes were fixed on the man in brightly-colored armor standing under a banner that hung limp as the wind died.

It was said later that the thunder of hooves from their mounted troops sounded like avenging gods. They rode straight at the shogun's forces, and Rikiko twirled her naginata so that it looked like the fierce rays of the sun descending upon them.

The front ranks broke under Rikiko's charge. The sweep of her blade parted heads from bodies, severed arms, rained blood down upon the already sodden ground. The shogun and his personal troops stood their ground, although the earth shook with battle.

No one knew, afterwards, where the arrow came from. It was fletched with the silver feathers of an eagle and seemed to drop down from the skies above. Certainly, Rikiko never saw the bolt that pierced her shoulder and threw her from her horse.

But her soldiers saw. They saw her fall, and it was as if their spirits were crushed as soon as Rikiko was knocked down. Exactly as her father had fallen.

She lay on the ground, surrounded by a knot of her co-conspirators, now all dismounted from their horses and clustered protectively around her. Her nephew Satoshi knelt beside her, and there were tears on his face mixed with the sweat and blood. A second man's shadow covered her face, and the man knelt down on her other side.

She blinked past the pain and looked up. Looked up to see the face of her sworn enemy, the most hated face in all the world. He was surrounded by his bodyguard, and she saw now that her allies were held captive by his soldiers. All but her nephew, who had not relinquished his post by her side.

"You fought bravely," said the shogun. He was near enough the same age as her, although she had only seen him from afar when making the alliances that ended the first war. He didn't smile, but, as he looked down at her, the edges of his eyes crinkled.

At that reminder of her father, she closed her eyes, knowing that tears were leaking from the corners of them. Through the blackness of her closed lids, she heard him say, "Because of your bravery, I will spare your heir's life, and yours, if you wish it. But you will never raise a naginata again, or you will die. Then your heir will die. And I will erase the name of Koizumi from the world. Do you understand?"

She remembered long ago her father telling her that the name of their family would echo through the centuries. Depending on her, it could end here and now.

Even though Tachibana was already gone. Gone forever, except for the one at her side. It could end here.

Or—despite everything she had already lost, it could go on.

She nodded, but didn't open her eyes. She felt a hand on her unwounded side grasping her shoulder, sealing the pact. Then it was gone.

Rikiko opened her eyes. Satoshi was still looking at her, still crying. "Aunt," he said, although the word broke in the middle and he had to repeat it.

She nodded again, her throat too tight for words.

"Let's go home," he said.

♦ ♦ ♦ REVENGE ♦ ♦ ♦

WHEN MARIA TURNED TO LOOK over her shoulder for the third time in as many minutes, George did also. "What is it?"

"Nothing," she said, too quickly. "Forget it. We'll be late to the party."

Out of the darkness, a low growl marched up from behind them. They walked faster, but the sound intensified. Up ahead where the streetlights had been knocked out, sudden flames appeared out of the darkness—glowing red eyes. A white body followed the eyes, teeth dripping strings of liquid.

"*Cadejo*," Maria breathed.

Before he could ask, the creature flowed towards them in a rush. From behind, the low growl became a ferocious snarl, and a black dog sailed over their heads to stop the white one in mid-leap. George grabbed Maria's hand and they ran, the snarls of the fight gradually fading into the distance.

Blood pounded through his temples as they reached the third floor of their building and he fumbled with the key before slamming his way inside their apartment. "What was that?" He locked the door behind them and leaned against it, panting.

Maria paced away from him, crossing herself. "Two brothers cursed for all eternity."

"What do you mean two brothers? They were *dogs*."

"Magic. Black magic," she said bitterly.

"You've got to be kidding."

"Kidding?" She turned back to him, rubbing her hands up and down her arms, as if cold. The white makeup around her eyes seemed garish now instead of fun, especially after the attack. Maria was dressed in an angel costume, with glitter trailing down her cheeks like silver tears. "Local legend is that my ancestors cursed the brothers to this form. Each generation, on the anniversary of their transformation, they compete with each other to take a tribute from my family in flesh and blood. I never believed the story before this —"

"Your father," George made the connection. "You said he was killed on Halloween."

She glanced away from him again. "My family warned me not to go out after my thirtieth birthday—oh, God, I wish I'd never let you convince me to go to the party—"

"It's okay," he murmured, his mind racing. His fear was fading already—he always knew Maria was superstitious, but she spoke so little about her past. It was hard to know if she was just being hysterical or if there was a deeper problem at play. Did she really believe what she was saying?

He stepped forward and took her into his arms, gently rubbing her back around her feathered white wings. Her halo pressed against his shoulder as she dropped her head against him, her shoulders shaking with grief.

But as he soothed her with quiet nonsense words and she started to relax, he heard something he shouldn't have, something incongruous, something impossible—he heard the creak of the front door, the door he had locked, being slowly pushed open behind him.

♦ ♦ GRANDMOTHER WINTER ♦ ♦

"IN THE FOREST LIVES AN old woman," said Ellie's mother. "She will eat you if you are bad. Mind me or else."

It was hard for Ellie to take her mother seriously. She was old enough to know the difference between the village superstitions and her mother's tales. But still, she said yes. She would watch her brother.

Once she agreed, her mother tied on a scarf and left Ellie standing in the doorway holding baby Jackson. The girl watched her mother walk out through the front gate without a backward glance at the two she left behind.

Jackson was especially fussy today. He cried as Ellie fed him sloppy porridge; he stole the spoon and threw it on the floor. Then he spit his meal up all over Ellie.

"Shh," she tried to soothe him. "Shh." His face brightened and swelled like a birthday balloon. She wanted to pop him, to deflate his puffed-out cheeks and screwed-up fists that batted at her. She wanted to leave him crying by himself and go off to play. He would cry whether she was there or not—she couldn't soothe him.

The sky darkened outside. Mother could take hours, wherever she went to. Ellie had asked several times if she could come along, but had been told no. "It's grown-up stuff," she was told the first time. "When you're older," the next time. Finally her mother screamed, "No! Stop asking!"

So she stopped.

Jackson wailed as she bounced him up and down in her arms. She pleaded with him, but he ignored her. She changed his diaper, but he peed on her. She sang a song while he hit her in the nose.

Her mother's words boiled up inside of her and she shouted, "No! Stop crying!"

This only made him squeeze more tears out and scream harder.

Finally, she put him in his crib and covered him in a blanket that he immediately kicked off. That was it—she couldn't take it anymore. She walked through the door and shut it behind her.

The air outside was still and heavy with electricity. The wooly clouds were dirty with potential, low and grey and grimy. Guilt filled her throat as she walked away, but she did not turn around. The back of her head crawled with the wrongness of Jackson left behind, alone and crying in his crib.

Ellie slunk into the trees, but didn't go far. Of course, she promised to some nameless entity inside her head, she would return in a minute and obey the summons of her brother's cries. Of course, she wouldn't leave him alone for long.

But she lingered at the edge of the woods. The trees leered at her with twig teeth, and she idled beneath them in a tortured mix of freedom and shame. Another minute and she would return to the house, rescue Jackson from his crib, and hold him until their mother returned. She would be good, after this next minute.

Or maybe this one.

Perhaps a couple more.

She watched the clouds swing over their house in the small clearing as she leaned her head back against the base of a large and knobby tree. The sky roiled like boiling soup and she huddled in her coat against the growing winds of the storm. Her coat was old and warm, too large for her by far. It had been her father's, her mother once told her, but would say no more about it.

Ellie closed her eyes against the wind and snuggled down inside the coat. She felt comforted by it, sheltered in a cocoon of her father's long-ago protection.

When she next opened her eyes, it was to darkness and wailing. She jumped to her feet. A confusion of thoughts tumbled through her head, until she remembered Jackson left alone in the house. Her mother would be livid at her for abandoning him, no matter that she had never left sight of their home.

Except… how could she have gotten so turned around? She looked left and right, but there was nothing but forest and more forest. There was no clearing, no small and familiar cottage. The branches of the trees loomed out of the darkness like the tales she had heard about sinister creatures of the woods, and Ellie remembered her mother threatening her before she left with the idea of the old woman of the forest.

The wailing was louder now, and Ellie was frightened until she realized it was the wind moaning through the branches. A rumble echoed through the sky, and the first cold drops fell down, white as the trees were black, the stark colors of nighttime.

She had no choice but to walk or freeze. Choosing a direction at random, she shuffled her feet forward, huddling inside her coat. The snow fell down, an endless kaleidoscope of sky demons dancing over her head. Her toes hurt, then numbed, and her feet lost feeling next. Still, she walked and the snow fell.

Her head was tucked down below the collar of her coat for warmth, and she was not sure what made her look up, but when she did, she saw a light flickering in the distance. *The clearing!* she thought gratefully. *Home.*

The idea filled her with longing, a visceral tug that sped her numb feet and spurred her to a careless speed. She tripped and sprawled on the ground, knocking away her breath. She lay flat on a bed of snow and struggled to take air in and out. The cold of the hard earth seeped up her arms and into her chest so that she coughed convulsively when she had recovered from the shock of the fall. *Can't lie here*, she thought and pushed to her feet. There was the light, her only hope of safety, and she walked forward again to follow it.

The light led her deeper into the woods. The trees were thicker, and the ephemeral brightness receded before her so she never got closer. In despair, she thought of will-o-the-wisps and what it would mean to be lost in the forest during a winter storm.

As if sensing her ragged emotions, the light flickered again and coalesced into a stable image. Ellie stumbled, fighting with the entwined branches that blocked her way. It seemed there was a clearing on the other side, but the trees were rooted fast and held firm against her numb fingers. She beat at them with her useless hands and shrieked wordlessly into the night.

At her cry, the branches suddenly gave way and she fell forward into a small, open area where the trees curved like a roof and bent around the sides of the space as tightly as a thicket. In the heart of the opening was a small cottage, just about the size of her home. Lights shone from all the windows but, oddly, the house looked like it was perched on a nest of dried sticks that elevated it up from the ground.

The wind howled and the snow blew against her back, urging her forward. Fear beat through her skull as hard as the fingers of the wind, yet she still hesitated despite the impetus of cold. Finally, she walked forward until she reached the door and knocked. It was a timid rap, but she could hear the echoes inside as if she had smote upon the door with all of her force.

Quite clearly, she heard a voice say, "Enter." The tone of the voice was as cold as the wind and chilled her through, much as the winter storm had. But she had come here and had no other choice, so she pulled the latch and stepped inside.

The warmth of the fire inside was overwhelming after the cold, and she felt the sting of heat on her face like a slap. She quietly closed the door behind her, her eyes drinking in the simple room. A trundle bed sat in the far corner by the fireplace and, in between the two, was a scarred table and chairs. An old woman sat in one of the chairs and she had a knife in her hand. It was as long as the woman's arm and she held it pointed at the door. No, pointed at *Ellie*.

"It's a cold night for a cold heart," said the woman. Then she laughed, splinters of ice edging through it. "What are you doing wandering the woods on such a night?"

"Please, ma'am, I got lost," Ellie said. She waited next to the door, dripping with melting snow, afraid to venture further. The woman put down the knife and smiled, but the smile brought no comfort. Her face was a nest of wrinkles and her mouth had few teeth. Around her neck was a string of long, off-white beads that tinkled strangely as she moved. "I beg of you, please let me stay here until the storm ends, and then I can be on my way."

"You beg for my care? You must have a kind heart to expect favors from a stranger. Do you care for others when they need you?"

Ellie's mind flashed back to her brother and her eyes pricked with guilty tears. "No, ma'am, I do not. My brother needed me, and I left him behind."

"Aha," said the old woman. "Well, I am not you. For the truth of your words and the regret in your heart, you are welcome to my fire and to share my meal."

Stunned by the generosity, Ellie blinked her eyes and the tears fell down. "Thank you." She swiped the back of her hand across her cheeks. "I will do whatever I can to repay you."

"Not a wise promise to give to a stranger in the woods," said the old woman. She stood, and Ellie could see that the old woman was small, no taller than herself. Perhaps the woman had once been larger, but her back was bent with age and her fingers gnarled with it. Still, she moved lightly across the floor to the fire and dished stew into two bowls from a pot suspended over the flames. She thunked them onto the worn surface of the table, and Ellie sat down across from her, feeling as if she were floating in a dream. Her fingers tingled with returning life.

"What is your name, girl?" asked the woman, giving her a spoon. Ellie told her and took a mouthful of the stew. It was so hot it seared her tongue. "Where is your family?"

After a hesitation while she took a bite and chewed it, Ellie told her this also. "So your mother left you alone? Where does she go when she is gone all day?"

"I don't know," said the girl. "She will not tell me."

"Hmm," said the old woman. By this time, Ellie had eaten her fill, and she felt warm and drowsy. Her eyelids began to droop and she had problems listening to the woman, despite trying to be polite.

"Come," said the voice. "I have blankets in that chest, there. You may sleep before the fire."

Ellie went where she was directed and curled herself into the blankets. Now warmed through, she fell asleep.

♦♦♦

When she woke, Ellie was in her own bed at home. She blinked sleep-furred eyes and glanced around. There, in his crib, was her sleeping brother. Her mother was in the bed next to her, also fast asleep.

Had it just been a dream? She sat up as gently as possible so as to not wake the baby, but was startled by the loud thud of something dropping to the floor. She froze. A rustle of cloth was followed the next minute by a thin wail as Jackson woke.

"Ellie!" grunted her mother, and the girl went and picked up her brother. As soon as she touched him, he quieted and looked at her. His blue eyes crinkled and he smiled. She felt her heartbeat racing in her chest and she held him tightly in her arms in apology for leaving him the day before.

But there had been the thump when she rose. Ellie turned

her head to look at the floor and bent to pick it up. It was heavier than it should be for something so small, and she stood there, Jackson propped on one shoulder, holding the item in her left hand. It filled her palm and glowed with the morning sun streaming through the windows.

Her mother stretched and said, yawning, "What have you got there?"

"A golden heart," Ellie answered in a whisper.

"A gold—what?" Her mother jumped to her feet and came around the bed. She snatched the object from her daughter's hands. She tested it with her fingernail and then her teeth. "Where did you find this?"

Ellie told her about the old woman in the woods. About how she had fallen asleep there and woken here, holding the golden heart in her hand. "An old woman," murmured her mother. "And she obviously gave you this—but why?" Ellie didn't know.

"Where there is one, there may be more," said her mother. "But I don't trust that you'll know how to get them. Watch Jackson. I'll be back."

So Ellie spent the day watching her brother. Whatever had ailed him before was gone, and they played with the golden heart, which he seemed to enjoy. She would roll it along the carpet, thumpety, thumpety, and he would laugh and clap his hands.

When darkness fell, their mother returned. "A waste of time!" she said, picking twigs from her hair. "I couldn't find the old woman's hut. Well, no matter, I will take the gold to town tomorrow to sell."

"You can't! It's mine," argued Ellie.

"No matter that it was yours. It's mine now. This means

that we can live well, better than we do now. Give it to me."

Ellie refused, but her mother overpowered her and snatched it away. "You wicked child!" she scolded. "The old woman of the forest will eat you for being bad!"

The girl said nothing. She got little sleep that night, knowing her mother would be selling her heart tomorrow.

Her mother was gone early and stayed away all day. When she returned, she was furious.

"No one will buy it! When I showed it to them, they just took one look at me and threw me from their store. Maybe they thought I stole it, or maybe it isn't gold after all. See, look at my hands. They have turned red from handling it, so something has rubbed off on me. But, no matter. If they won't take it from my hands, maybe they will take it from yours," she told Ellie. "Tomorrow, you will come to town with me and sell it."

"I won't," said Ellie, holding Jackson. Her mother moved to take the baby, but Jackson howled and clung to his sister.

"Fine then, see how you like going hungry!" snapped her mother. "If you won't sell it, then you both can starve."

The next morning, their mother packed up all the food in the house and carried it with her to town, not once glancing back over her shoulder at the two children standing in the doorway watching her leave. As the hours passed, Jackson cried and Ellie could give him only water from the well to fill his belly. With her own stomach snarling at her, she warmed the golden heart between her hands, and an idea suddenly came to her. Quickly, she bundled up the baby and herself and walked into the woods carrying Jackson.

The trees seemed to bow down before her as she walked and Jackson became quiet. He watched the winter sky, which showed clear blue through the sere branches. Before long, they were at the house in the heart of the woods and Ellie knocked on the door. "Enter," said the cold voice.

The room was much the same as before. The old woman lowered her knife and put it on the table when she saw them, but said nothing in greeting. "I have returned with my brother," explained Ellie under the watchful eyes of the old woman. "And I come to thank you for the gift."

"What gift?" asked the woman guilelessly, then laughed. "I see you are both hungry. Come, there is much in my stew pot today." She put bowls before them and watched as Ellie fed her brother the soft vegetables in the broth first before touching her own stew. After Jackson was done eating, he played on the floor with the wooden spoon from the pot.

The girl ate steadily and looked at the old woman's necklace. It was yellow and made of long, thin beads, as if it were made from bones, and the image reminded her of her mother's threats about the dangers of the woods and old women who ate children. Before she could scare herself, Ellie looked away from the necklace and tried to think only of the warmth and the comfort of the food which filled her empty stomach.

"You have a long journey home," said the old woman when she was finished. "But you are always welcome here."

"Thank you, ma'am," said Ellie.

"Call me Grandmother," said the old woman.

"Thank you, Grandmother," she said dutifully. Smiling, the old woman gestured them on their way.

The trip back didn't seem so long, and the trees nodded at them as they passed. When they got home, their mother was waiting and her face darkened when she saw them. "Where have you been?" she demanded. When Ellie told her, their mother ripped at her own hair in frustration. "Show me this path in the woods!"

So Ellie pointed to where she had walked through the forest, and watched her mother run off into the gathering twilight. The girl put Jackson to bed, rekindled the fire, and waited. Eventually, her eyes grew heavy and she fell asleep.

When she woke, the first thing she saw was a kettle hanging over the flames of the fireplace. The pot gleamed as bright as moonlight and the smell coming from it made her mouth water. Jackson must have smelled it too, for he was sitting up in his crib, clutching at the bars and staring at her. She took him out and fed him broth from the pot, and then ate herself. She had never tasted anything so wonderful. The meat was tender and juicy, the vegetables as flavorful as if they had just been pulled from the earth. Jackson laughed and clapped his hands.

The door opened just as she finished eating and her mother stormed in, her hair a rats' nest. There were scratches on her face, as if she had tried to claw her way through branches and been clawed in return. Her palms were still bright red from when she had touched Ellie's golden heart and she sniffed the air until she located the silver pot on the fire. The woman let out a shriek and advanced on the stewpot. "Where did you get this?"

Ellie told her about waking to find it there. Her mother dipped a ladle of it into a bowl and began to eat, but she spit it out after several mouthfuls and went gagging to the door. Ellie glanced in the bowl – a wriggling worm bobbed to the surface and then dipped back down into the soup.

"What trick is this, you nasty child?" said their mother on

her return. She hauled the silver pot out the door and dumped its contents in the woods. "I will take the pot to town to sell," she said, straightening her hair.

Ellie stayed silent. She was unsurprised when their mother returned that afternoon, ranting and raving and still carrying the pot. Her mouth was colored a bright green that she swore came from the stew she had eaten and vomited. Between her red hands and green face, she looked like a holiday decoration.

"Tomorrow morning, I will follow you into the woods," she said. "And we will see how that old biddy does, then."

And that is what happened. Morning came, and Ellie carried Jackson into the woods. The trees let the two children through easily and their mother pushed in behind them, even though the snarled branches tried to block her way. When they came to the clearing, Ellie almost hoped that the house would be gone or some other such magic, but there it stood, perched upon its pile of twigs. The old woman's voice called out when the girl knocked and the three of them went into the house.

"Hello, Grandmother," said Ellie.

"Don't 'Grandmother' her," said her mother. "I want answers."

"Answers, hmm," said the old woman. "I will answer your questions. But, for each you ask, I will ask one also."

"Fine," her mother said shortly. "Why have you given Ellie such wealthy gifts?"

"Gifts?" said the old woman. "I have given her nothing from my hands except food and shelter when she was lost and hungry. You may have the same, if you wish."

"But what about the heart and the kettle? Where did they come from?"

"I think," said the old woman, "it is my turn for a

question."

"Very well."

"Where do you go when you leave the children?"

"That is none of your business!" said their mother.

"Answer the question. Speak truly." The old woman's voice was cold.

"I go nowhere."

"Hmm," said the old woman. "Now it is your turn."

"Why will no one buy the gold and silver?" she asked.

"Because they are not yours to sell."

"But how would they know that?"

"My turn," said the woman.

"Ask, then!" shouted their mother.

"Who is the father of these children?"

"I don't know," answered their mother, growing pale.

"Hmm," said the old woman. "Now ask your last question."

"This can't be my last question! I have a lot more questions to ask."

"Nevertheless, this is your last one. Choose it carefully."

"Fine." Their mother stared at the old woman, as if she could divine her secrets with the force of her gaze. "Then this is my question. What can I do to get your riches?"

"You can't," said the old woman. "For I have none. I already told you that I gave no gifts. All my possessions are in this room that you see. Now, for my last question. Who is the mother of these children?"

Their mother turned the color of the snow outside. "I am. That is enough, old woman."

"You are right. It is enough." And with one quick movement, the old woman threw her knife across the room and straight through their mother's heart.

Ellie screamed and nearly dropped the baby. Jackson, feeling his sister's distress, started to sob, while the impaled woman hit the floor with a noise like stones falling. Ellie turned horrified eyes from their mother's body to the old woman, who had not moved from her spot in the chair. The girl cried, "Is this my punishment for leaving Jackson? I promised not to do it again! How could you take our mother from us?"

"Hush, child," said the old woman in the voice of winter. "I have taken nothing from you. That woman was no mother of yours. Not one word she spoke in this room was true."

"But… she raised me. She brought Jackson home to be a brother to me," Ellie said.

"If you were older, you would know that children are not brought home, like a parcel from the marketplace. She stole you away from your real parents and kept you hidden so that she could gain money by promising to return you. You are not the child of that woman. You have a mother and a father who have never stopped wishing to see you again. And your brother is no brother to you. He was taken the same way from his parents."

"No," Ellie sobbed. "Why? Why has this happened?"

"It is the way of wickedness," answered the old woman. "The wicked shall fall before the just. Now, you must return to your family and the baby must return to his." She got to her feet and made her creaking way over to the two of them. Ellie clutched Jackson fiercely to her.

"No! You can't take him away from me. He's mine."

"Child," said the woman. "He belongs to himself. You must let him go."

"I love him!" she cried. "He's my brother. He's all I have."

"Aha!" And with that, the old woman bent over and dipped her finger into the blood pooling under the dead woman. She raised her hand and touched a dot of the blood to each child's forehead. Ellie was too shocked to resist.

"*Stupay s Bogom*," said the old woman. And then the room swirled up around the two children, a whirlwind that encompassed them. When the winds died, the children were gone.

The old woman looked down at the body on the floor and knelt beside it to retrieve her knife. She used the blade to make the first cuts, cleanly and clinically. She had to steady herself as the house stood up on its large and spindly feet, stretching legs like an oversized fowl. Then the cottage shouldered its way out through the grasping trees, taking steps that shook the forest with their power. Using a direction known only to itself, it headed for the place they would be needed next.

She worked as quickly as she could. By tonight, there needed to be more meat for her stew pot.

♦ ♦ ♦ A Body at Rest ♦ ♦ ♦

THE MAN WAS STARING AT her again. Riva stood at the sink washing dishes and saw him standing in the shade of the trees outside the kitchen window.

"Mum," she said.

"What now?" asked her mother, chopping vegetables for stew.

"Nothing," Riva said after a pause. Her mother came up behind her and peered over her shoulder. The man was standing there and staring at Riva, but her mother's eyes scanned the scene without pausing. After a moment, her mother went back to her chopping.

"Don't bother me over nothing," she said.

"Yes, Mum."

On laundry day at the end of the week, the two of them were outside scrubbing linens with water hauled up from the stream, heated in a pot over the fire, and poured into the wash basins. Her mother had gone inside, and Riva was just hanging up the last wet sheet when she lost her grip and the end whipped past her face. Looking beyond it, she saw the man standing not ten feet from her.

She froze, her hands outstretched still to tangle with the unwieldy sheet. He smiled; his teeth were glaring white.

Her mouth was open to say something, but the sheet whipped back around in the breeze and slapped her across the face. As she grabbed ahold of it, she knew before she lowered it that he would have disappeared.

She left her empty basket where it lay and walked towards the woods. Although she knew enough about husbandry to distinguish a poisonous plant from a useful one, she didn't recognize the flower she found in the place where the man had been standing. She knelt down by the plant, hesitating at the thorns twined about its stem. The scent of the bloom was strange and intoxicating, and she found herself grabbing the flower and ripping it from its nest of leaves. As she did so, one of the thorns pricked her, so that a single drop of blood fell to the earth. She put the wound to her mouth and sucked on it. The taste was bitter on her tongue, leaving an uneasy feeling behind.

Still, she carried the flower inside the house with her. That night, she placed it under her pillow and slept with its sweet fragrance drifting around her. Her dreams were vivid and troubling, but forgotten upon waking.

In the morning, the temperature dropped dramatically as it sometimes did in the middle of spring. She wore her petticoats doubled and her thickest woolen cloak when she went to fetch water from the stream. After the chores were done, her mother declared she was setting off for town.

"I won't be long," she warned her daughter.

Riva knew she should complete the list of chores her mother had given her, but instead she retrieved the flower from under her pillow. Holding it in one hand, she walked into the woods where she had last seen the man.

Her bare feet seemed guided by Providence, and she avoided rocks and sharp twigs with ease. She pulled her cloak tightly around her and her breath frosted the air around her.

When she broke through into a small clearing, the sudden touch of sunlight on her head woke her up. She turned to look behind her, but the trees crowded at her back and their intertwined branches seemed impenetrable. Fear shivered through her.

"Riva," said a voice. It was lilting, reminding her of the folk songs patterned after the staccato of falling rain. She turned her head and there he was in the bright sun with her, a million jewels of light glinting in his midnight hair. He held a hand out to her and she reached out her own fingers, noticing only at the last moment that she had extended her arm with the hand holding the flower. He smiled and grasped her hand, flower and all, and the petals were crushed between their two palms.

She felt a flicker of pain—thorns, piercing her skin. It failed to wake her from the trance of the man's touch. Something on the edge of her thoughts hinted about the dreams of the night before, but the memory did not come fully forward. She closed her eyes against the brilliance of the day.

With his hand, he drew her closer. The light flickered against her eyelids.

There was movement and sensation, both overwhelming. Then the night descended, a darkness covering everything with its touch.

♦♦♦

Riva opened her eyes, and the world was soft-edged and overlapped by shadows. She pushed against the ground, and her bones snicked and clacked in a painful manner. Although she managed to draw herself upwards, tendon and sinew protested every action. As her head lifted from the ground, there was a slithering sound like a hundred snakes, and she looked at the grass and saw a rushing towards her of . . . *something*. A weight pulled against her head and she realized the endless coils were attached to her, a nest of hair entwined in the groundcover of the clearing. Her hair, endless loops and curls, tight and painful on her scalp. Her neck strained, but she managed to pull herself up eventually and found herself sitting upright in the center of a sea of tarnished yellow.

Even so simple a move exhausted her. She sat still for a while, noting the trees ringing the space where she was. The clearing was much as she remembered it, but the day was warm now and her rucked-up petticoats too hot.

A voice interrupted her wandering thoughts. Just her name. She turned her head and the dark-haired man appeared in her line of vision.

Her mouth was dry and her tongue fumbled as she tried to make sounds. “Hush,” said the man and she found herself closing her mouth.

A youth stepped out from the trees and stopped next to the man. He was in that awkward stage consisting of doorknob-shaped elbows and knees, limbs stretched thinly between the knobby joints. There was something strange about the boy, but the light was poor and she couldn't see him well in the growing darkness.

The man bowed once, a courtly gesture that seemed oddly natural in the clearing. Then he faded backwards. She blinked and there was only a hollow space where he had been. The boy remained behind, staring at her.

"H-help," she croaked. The boy's eyes darted up to the crown of her head, and he drew a knife from his pocket, frightening her for just one moment—until he knelt beside her and sawed at the strands trapping her to the ground. By the time he was finished, it was full dark and the moon had not yet appeared.

Too dark to go anywhere, she thought. The boy watched her—she could see his eyes gleaming in the dark, like a cat's eyes reflecting and amplifying the dim light of the stars.

She tried to say, "Sit," but her voice failed her. Still, he seemed to understand, for he sank to the ground next to her.

Although she had done nothing so far, weariness filled her. She didn't try to speak again, simply lay back into the hollow where she had woken, a curious bare patch of earth sunken slightly into the ground. Curling up, she pillowed her head on her crossed hands and fell asleep.

♦ ♦ ♦

Light woke her, or perhaps the sound of birds trilling softly nearby. She turned her head and saw the boy. He was upright and watching her, as if he hadn't moved all night. His gaze felt like ants creeping on her skin, and she shivered in the warm light of the dawn. The sun was behind him, but she could see enough to notice there was something wrong with his eyes—one was pale as cheese, the other a dark black. Instead of giving him a quizzical look as one might expect, it made him seem dangerous, as if he were a wild beast come to stare at her, considering whether or not to take her for a meal.

Her mouth was still dry, but she found that she could speak. "Let's go home."

The boy said nothing, but he stood when she stood and followed her out of the clearing. She headed south, the woods familiar to her, the trees like old friends who nodded gently as she passed them. Eventually, she noticed a large tumble of boulders she knew was near to her house. With a glad cry, she turned slightly to orient herself and began to walk more quickly. When she came to the stream, she knelt to drink. Hunger was nothing new to her, so she ignored the grumbling in her stomach that accompanied the weight of the liquid in it. Instead, she turned her head and saw the boy kneeling beside her and scooping up the water to drink.

The action was so normal that she relaxed. She wondered why he was with her, why the man had led him to her. But more than her curiosity about him was a homesickness that clogged her throat and stopped her from asking. He followed her without protest as she stood and moved off along the bank of the stream.

She'd been thinking her own thoughts, letting her feet choose their way for a while before she realized they should've already broken free from the trees and into the clearing where she lived with her mother. Perhaps she'd been so caught up in her thoughts that she hadn't seen it? However, if they continued on, they would eventually reach the village. She often made toys for the children there, carved out of bits of deadfall from the forest. The mothers were fond of her; perhaps they would give the two of them something to eat and find a place for the strange boy.

They walked on, the stream gurgling beside them. Each moment, she kept thinking they would come out of the trees and see the village. Her legs were tired, her stomach clenching with hunger. *Perhaps now*, she thought, again and again.

Her heart thudded in her chest when she realized the light was fading. They had been walking for hours. She sank down to her knees and was suddenly angry when the boy squatted beside her. What could he know about disappearing houses, vanishing towns? The stream was the same, she was sure of it. But her home was gone, and the village also.

Pain lanced through her middle. "I'm so hungry," she whispered.

The boy stood up and walked away. She watched dully as he disappeared between one tree and the next. The comfort she had found in the forest at the beginning of the day disappeared beneath a sharp stab of fear. A night bird screamed in the distance and her breath hitched.

She waited as the shadows deepened. The texture of the night was muffled under the trees, the darkness closing down over her head and pressing against her sodden heart. Perhaps she would have cried, but she felt too exhausted to try. Instead, she sat on the cool ground, numb and unsleeping.

Movement in the woods, and her heart knocked against her throat. She didn't recognize the boy until he stood right before her, for he was a shapeless figure in the deeper shadow of the trees. He held something out to her, but she couldn't tell what it was until her hands dropped beneath the weight of his offering. It was a hare, neck flopping against her hands.

She placed the offering on the ground beside her—nothing to be done with it in the dark. "Thank you," she said softly. The boy sat down beside her. Eventually, between one breath and the next, her head fell forward and she slept.

She woke with a sharp pain in her neck when she moved it. "A bed," she murmured. "A quilt. Food . . ." And then she remembered the hare.

They had nothing to make a fire. She skinned the creature with the boy's knife and they ate what she could scrape off its lean bones. Afterwards, she washed the blood off her hands in the stream and took a long drink before they continued on their way.

She no longer knew where to go. But there was no reason to stop. So she walked on, and the boy followed.

On the third day, it rained. Her dress was filthy from travel and ragged from scraping against tree branches. The cloth stuck to her skin and she felt even dirtier than before because of the heat and wet. "Ugh," Riva said to the boy. "I wish we could—"

A crack of thunder interrupted her words, and she couldn't breathe. She tried to say something, anything, but found the world had frozen around her. The ground reached out and smacked her in the back of the head, which made the pain in her chest even worse. If she had any breath, she would have cried out. But it seemed she could not speak.

The boy bent over her. His hands were on her face and she saw he was moving his mouth. She wanted to laugh—here she was, speechless, and him trying to say something. A reversal.

"Mother," she heard him say in a voice like a lilting song. His fingers caressed her face and the look in those strange eyes made her heart pause. Weary, she closed her eyes.

♦♦♦

The hunter came out of the woods and his gun dropped from his fingers. He covered his mouth with one hand. There, a teenage boy bent over an old woman on the ground. Her chest was red and wet, like a gaping mouth.

The boy turned his head toward the intruder on the scene, and the hunter stopped with his phone halfway out of his pocket. He had been about to call 9-1-1, but there was something off about the boy, something that gave him pause. The boy's great eyes blinked at the hunter and the man heard, unbelievably, an animal growl rising from that thin chest. He half-turned back to reach for his gun.

He never made it. Many years later, the gun was found by a child playing by the water, who stared at it curiously. Grown round by vines and carried up the trunk of a tree, the ancient rifle pointed straight upwards, mute testament to an outmoded practice. Guns were now irrelevant, a strange thing of the past. But the rifle stood sentinel still, as if to shoot at the blue, blue sky of heaven.

♦ THE GODMOTHER'S BARGAIN ♦

MY MOTHER DIED SO THE magic would work. She accidentally killed herself, cutting too deeply into her pulse points and sprinkling too much of her own blood throughout the garden as she tried to summon the spirit. I found her underneath the weeping willows, white as bone, with the blade fallen from her slack hand and standing sentinel over her body.

Although I didn't know what she planned, last night I dreamed about the spirit she summoned. I did as the dream told me, and I buried my mother's blade deep in the gardens underneath the willow trees. I dragged her body up to her chamber and disguised her self-inflicted wounds with paste and blood, creating suppurating sores, before running through the house crying plague. No one was brave enough to come close and see if I told the truth. Even my father wouldn't check on his "beloved" wife, stopped by fear of the deadly disease.

And I? I was daubed with the same brush as she, cast temporarily down into the servants' quarters in case I disturbed the household with my exposure to my mother's phantom illness. My costly furs and velvets stayed in my rooms, and I dressed in brown homespun clothes and slept next to the coals in the fireplace. The servants would not come near me other than when summoned, so the warm hearth was mine alone.

The night of my mother's death, I closed my eyes in exhaustion and fell instantly asleep. I saw my mother dancing underneath the willow trees, her arms and face were frozen in the rictus of death I had found her, but her legs limber and leaping like a deer. As she spun away, I saw she'd been dancing with a shadow under the weeping trees. The shadow moved toward me in a rush and I held out my hands—whether to stop it or welcome it, I did not know. I opened my mouth to speak, to scream, to stop it,—

—and woke on the hearth, my face smudged by the ashes of the fire.

Weeks passed and no one in the household fell ill. I was allowed to return to my old rooms. It wasn't long afterward my father introduced me to my new "mother."

Her face was round and plump, like a dairy maid's. I had seen her before with my father at odd moments, receiving a stolen kiss in the marketplace, greeting him in a doorway across the square. She moved into the house, along with her two daughters, one of which had my father's eyes, the other his short beak of a nose. It was not long before they were sheltered under my father's name.

"When it happens, do not hesitate," my mother told me the night before she unwittingly took her own life.

And I didn't hesitate. When the time was right, I struck, and the old man died.

It was that shrew mistress who suspected me. She was never so easy with my father's sudden death. She tried to keep me as far from her daughters as possible, but it was hard to isolate me without exposing her suspicions. She did her best, keeping me away from the lessons her daughters took, engaging a separate tutor for me. From the outside, one would think she cared.

"How you must mourn your father's death," she said, and had my meals sent to my room instead of allowing me at the table. "You need space to grieve in your own way."

In my bedchamber, I ate the food she sent and laughed softly to myself.

It wasn't until after my father's death that everything began to unravel. But by then, it was too late to save anyone.

♦♦♦

In my sleep, I danced as my mother had danced. When I woke abruptly, the household was silent. Outside the window, the gardens were lit as bright as daylight, it seemed. It was midnight, and when I stood, my limbs felt as languorous as if I were still sleeping. I moved in a dream down the stairs and through the kitchen, my bare feet making no sound. I stepped over the sleeping servants, the whisper of my fine lawn gown brushing over twitching faces that did not wake.

Out in the garden, the cold ground on the soles of my feet seemed to pierce through the mood. The cold traveled up my calves and into my thighs and seemed to lodge in my heart. With the chill, I remembered from my dream what I had to do.

Under the midnight moon, I danced in the gardens where my mother had died. From the outside, I was a pale slip of a girl, barely a threat to the deep shadows of the night. Inside, I had my purpose drilled into me from the moment I could walk and talk, the culmination of my mother's life. Underneath my feet, the earth that had drunk my mother's blood, that had witnessed her final summoning, shifted and groaned as if from great pressure.

The magic did not work for her, but then again, she was the first sacrifice.

It worked for me.

When I turned in the final circle, I saw a figure resting on a bench beneath the willow trees. The moon didn't penetrate the stark shadows of the drooping branches, so the figure was simply a darker hue against the black. There was something wrong about its outline, something that sucked at what little light might have exposed it, that trapped the moon's gentle glow in a miser's fist and released only more darkness.

"Godmother," I said in jest, and the figure threw back its head and laughed in great and violent joy. I shivered at the sound but didn't dare retreat. "I have a boon to ask you."

"You ask for a gift? But who will pay the price?"

Startled, I replied, "I have already paid."

Laughter again, but gentler, like a mother's indulgent chuckle. "Oh, child, you understand nothing. You have paid *nothing*."

"Fine." I raised my chin. "What is the price? I will pay it."

The shadow studied me, but I saw it finally nod. "You will." Fingers chopped through the air, cutting the light into pieces. "Give me your hand."

I took a deep breath. Although I had come this far, I did not trust what might happen next. But there did not seem to be many options open to me with such a direct order. I walked forward, keeping my eyes centered on the darker shadows of the willow trees. I held out my hand, palm forward.

A touch, so gentle I might have imagined it, and for a second, nothing.

Then a flood poured through me. Behind my closed eyelids, I saw images flickering in quick succession, so bright and fast they made little sense at first. Magic roared through my veins, battered my senses. My mouth was open, an endless scream escaping into the night, but the scream was as soundless as if I had been muzzled.

I found myself flat on my back staring up at the cold moon. My body felt bruised but filled with a power both dark and thrilling.

"That's the payment? Destroy the king?" I managed to croak in a voice that sounded ancient with knowledge.

A voice rustled from the shadows. "I have given you what you asked. Find my payment, then return to me. You have a month until I come looking for *you*."

♦♦♦

A lifetime marked out in the space of a month. The next morning, my stepmother came across me in the kitchens. She glanced around.

"What are you doing here? Where are the servants?"

"I dismissed them." At her shocked, rounded "o" of a mouth, I said, "I told them it was you who ordered it, and withheld their final wages. No one will take a position with us now. Well, what are you going to do?"

She stared at me for one long moment. Her eyes were dark, her brow furrowed. Without a word, she turned and stormed away.

I stayed in the kitchen. When midday came, I brought up to their rooms a tray of food for my half-sisters, a meal I had lovingly prepared with my own hands. Just as they sat down to eat, my stepmother came rushing into the room and knocked the food to the floor.

In a low voice, she hissed at me, "Try as you might, I will not allow you to do what your wicked heart desires. It is over. You have won."

"Won?" I asked with a smile. "Whatever do you mean?"

"I found what you wanted me to find—the newly turned earth in the garden. Five rows for the five servants you 'dismissed.' We will take ourselves from here. Immediately. Girls, pack only the bare essentials. We are going."

"Where will we go?"

"Why?" cried my half-sisters at the same time.

"It doesn't matter where we go, but go we must. For our lives. For our *souls*." The adulteress hustled the girls past me, making the sign of the cross as she did so.

♦♦♦

The following day, a knock boomed at the door of my empty house. Dressed in castoff rags left behind by one of the servants, I answered the summons. Smothered in gold braid, a man bowed stiffly to me and unrolled a scroll without pausing to raise his eyes to my unworthy demeanor.

"His Royal Highness, King George, requests the attendance of all the noble ladies of the kingdom for their celebration of Prince Frederick's natal day this evening." The messenger bowed once more, spun on his heel, and strutted off.

I had to wait until the sun disappeared, until the last light left the sky. Whereas poison worked at any time of day, magic—*my* magic—did not. Once darkness covered the earth like a smothering blanket, I pulled the magic into my service, creating from the cursed garden a veritable wealth of accoutrements. From the branches of the weeping willow, I spun a dress that draped around me like sorrow. From the tears cried in the garden by my stepsisters for our father, I fashioned two glass-clear slippers. From a death cap mushroom, I created a gleaming white carriage. Bats descended from the sky and I transformed them into midnight-black horses that moved in odd, jerking movements, as if trying to take flight.

My arrival at the castle gates did not go unnoticed. Whispers followed me into the palace, followed me as the prince came across the ballroom floor as if entranced and took my hand, while his father, the king, beamed at us from the dais. The prince and I danced all night, long past the setting of the moon. It was not until the air grew moist before dawn, not until I noticed the sky had not quite lightened, that I felt my magic begin to drain away. The sun would kill it completely, but before that happened, there was one more thing to accomplish.

I cast a spell over the crowd like a net. They closed their eyes and turned away for a moment as I walked up to the dais and took the long blade from beneath my skirts—the same blade that had killed my mother I had just dug up from the gardens that night—and I sunk it deep within the breast of the king.

By the time the crowd blinked and turned back to the dais, I was back across the room with the prince. Like the rest, I feigned shock and grief.

After the tedium of the king's funeral and a brief period of mourning, the prince and I were married. But by then, of course, he was king, crowned in a dazzling ceremony that anticipated only our wedding for its splendor.

After my husband fell asleep on our wedding night, I took the blade back and buried it in my father's gardens under the cold light of the moon.

"The price has been paid!" I danced as I had before, following in my mother's footsteps, and the shadows gathered under the willow.

Laughter rang through the gardens like a midnight bell, overwhelming me with the coldness of a thousand hating hearts.

"Oh, my little queen, you are wrong. You have failed."

My mouth dropped open in shock. "Failed? But . . . the king! I killed him. You told me must destroy the king."

"And yet the king still lives."

"What? That is not the same king! You cannot really expect me to kill everyone with royal blood. Why, even *I* am distantly related."

I saw the task stretching out before me, an impossible and unsolvable problem.

"The king is dead," said the voice, mocking me, fading back into the shadows. "Long live the king."

♦ ♦ ♦ LIQUID ♦ ♦ ♦

I.

IN THE WITCHING HOUR, MOONLIGHT skates over the gentle waters of the pond and touches on the weeping man on the bank. It swirls through algae, over sleeping fish, down to the heart of the waters.

The heart beats—once, twice. A shape emerges from the fluid, blinking midnight eyes, tossing back hair as dark as the oily tadpoles which float near the meniscus of the surface. Arms, breasts, toes, are birthed steaming into the cold night air.

When the man sees her, she draws him, unresisting, to her newborn body. With midnight magic, he is healed.

She is riven in two.

The stars fade, and the man walks away into the glowing haze of sky unfolding over the mountains—sunrise. He has been reborn, free of sorrow. The man's loafers leave imprints like question marks in the soft mud of the bank as he disappears. The pain of the light drives her back into the waters.

II.

When night returns the moon from behind the trees, it has the taste of freedom. She steps out from the water and doesn't look back.

As she walks under the shadows of trees, she loses her mother moon through blackened branches. A deer raises its head as she passes, its moon-eyes kin to her. It bows its head back to the grass, so little does she disturb the wildness of its heart.

The trees fall back—a spear of light accelerates from the edge of the mountains. It is joined by another strike of light, and yet another. Soon the horizon is glowing in shades of flesh—it tastes like fear on her tongue.

Come, urges the earth beneath her feet. She kneels and uses her hands like spades, scrabbling in the dirt. *Hurry*.

She covers herself with dirt and grasses and closes her eyes. Sleeping, there is a terrible heat seeking her, reaching out its fingers and plucking at her newborn water-skin.

III.

Coolness comes, and a return to shadows. She rises from the earth like a night-blooming flower.

Open space presses down around her—stars flicker and weave into rich patterns, like the shifting glow of the pond's surface. She looks up and feels the draw of her birthplace far behind her now.

The woman walks, and time flows away. Suddenly—horror returns, reflected across the sky in streamers of light. She paws at the dirt, and the earth swallows her, greedy. Although her eyes are closed, she is melting down again, drip by drip, from the hunger of the sun.

IV.

When the stars cry out softly, she dances and laughs beneath the mother moon. Grasses brush her breasts, her arms, her thighs.

It is the fourth night. The time of change.

In drunken wonder, she has forgotten everything—herself, her footsteps, the call she follows. She has become *now*, and she dances to the music of the crickets and tree frogs who serenade her.

The night sings softly in defeat as it fades away. Pink bleeds into the sky, but the fear goes untasted, unremembered—it is no longer real, no longer a shade held between the two of them.

The sun rises.

It pierces through her in a glorious ecstasy of pain. She feels her new lover filling her with the power of his form, a burning heat spreading out from the center of her body. She wraps her arms around him and throws back her head.

The sun rises.

She remembers love—and loss—as shafts of light move through her.

The sun rises.

She lets go.

V.

Moonlight touches the waters of a pond and a girl crying on the edge of the bank. The white light swirls down to the heart of the waters, dripping through the liquid like cold fire.

Once, twice—a sound echoes through the witching hour.

A heart beats.

♦ ♦ ♦ AFTER WAR ♦ ♦ ♦

THE BABY BLINKED AND FOCUSED her eyes on the King. Without fumbling, she reached out and clasped the fingers of his hand in a grip strong enough to hurt, as strong as a man's. From that moment, the King knew his daughter was a gods-blessed offering to the Moga.

"Battle," said the King's seer. The woman closed her eyes and swayed under the weight of prophecy. "This little one will be the center of it."

And so he named her Guerrière, princess of war. When she learned how to walk, her father handed her a javelin to lean on. When she learned how to run, he outfitted her with armor so she could carry a burden and stay fleet of foot. Her first spoken word was "spear."

But with her fate hanging so heavily upon her, no one stopped to question what the princess wanted. The King's eyes, when he turned them towards her, saw only the armor and the spear. They did not see anything else.

♦♦♦

"What is the matter, Gueri?"

She'd managed to evade her guard, Amadou, for half the morning. She'd slipped out of the compound before the sun rose, when he was nodding off over his spear, and stole as quietly as an antelope into the open savannah. She'd walked until the sun was a handspan in the sky, and then rested under the shade of a shea tree, simply sitting and watching the grasses move. She had brought no weapon with her.

Amadou's voice was not unexpected. He was a talented tracker and had taught her all that he knew. She was aware he'd be able to find her, only surprised it had taken him so long. He was not so young as he used to be, and she wondered if her father would find a replacement for him soon.

"War, war, and more war." She waved a hand out at the open space. "I want a morning to see the sun rise."

Amadou settled heavily beside her. "The sun rises every day," he replied. "It rose yesterday and it will rise tomorrow."

"But I want to see it *today*." She jumped to her feet, agile as a dancer. "Maybe I will not see it tomorrow."

"Ah." Amadou rubbed his chin with one hand, his spear resting in the crook of his arm. "Certainly you will not, if you do not continue with your training."

Gueri snorted. "Is that all there is, then? Training and war?"

Amadou laughed. "You are young, Gueri. There is more. But those two things—yes, that is what will come to you first."

Her eyes were dark as she glared at him. "Is there anything after war?"

"That," said Amadou, groaning to his feet, "is up to your father to tell you."

♦♦♦

"No."

"Why not? At my age, Mother was married to you. Why can I not marry?"

"Because I said so."

"That is no reason."

"I am your father and the King! When I tell you no, you will obey."

Gueri looked down at her feet. She scuffed her boot against the ground. "What if—"

"No more questions!" roared her father.

She turned and left the room.

♦♦♦

Gueri couldn't remember a time when weapons felt strange in her hands. When she picked up a spear, javelin, knife or bow, they were like extensions of her arm, her body. She'd grown accustomed to armor on her back in the hot sun—in fact, she felt naked without it. In her dreams, she heard the thunder of hooves. Tactics was the only thing she needed to learn, and she did so grudgingly—when to fall back, when to advance, when to set a trap, all the minutiae of thinking ahead that didn't come naturally to her. It took time to wrap her head around the intricacies of solid strategy, rather than just running at the enemy and fighting until they were killed.

Shortly after her conversation with her father about marriage, they were interrupted at their meal when outriders came roaring into camp. The sentries, briefly outnumbered, began to fall back. Despite the screams outside, Gueri did not hesitate. She snatched up her spear and bow where they had been resting next to her on the ground, and was the first out the door, ahead even of her father.

The scene that met her eyes was confusion. Men struggled back and forth with each other, knives pressed together, blood dripping onto the dirt. Figures loomed out of the raised dust, so that as she strode forward, eyes intent on the conflict, she nearly fell over a man prone on the ground, his body bristling with arrows. She dropped her bow at the door to the compound—it would be useless with such low visibility—and ran up to the nearest man-to-man fight. With a smooth turn of her wrist, she stabbed the foreign tribesman through the side. Oumarou, the sentry whom he'd been fighting, was winded, but able to nod his thanks to her as he bent over to catch his breath. She spun at a sound behind her and nearly jammed her spear through her father, pulling back just in time.

"Come," he said, eyeing her weapon warily. She nodded and followed him quickly through the clouds of dust. Ahead, the shouts and screams grew louder, the dust retreating behind them until the true battle was revealed.

Amadou was waiting for them, holding the reins of their horses. Without a word, they mounted and rode to war.

♦♦♦

Years later, it was still that first battle that woke her from sleep. Although other fights blurred in her memory—faceless men, the smell of blood and worse things—that first battle always remained clear in her head. People she'd known all her life died in front of her, and she dealt wounds close enough to see the light leave the eyes of the men she stabbed. At the time, she felt scared and a little numb—she was fighting for survival, for her people, for all the reasons drilled into her since she was young. It was only later that she had time to think about it, and time to remember.

The only thing that seemed unclear afterwards was how long the battle took. They had been eating their morning meal when attacked, but by the time the dust settled and only the groans of the wounded remained after the tumult of fighting, the sun was orange and baleful as it descended. Hours must have passed in what felt like seconds, although she suddenly noticed blood dripping from several wounds on her calves and one cut on her arm, realized the pain of her injuries only after she saw them. In a heartbeat, her arms felt like stone, and it was all she could do to rein her mount around and head back at a weary trot towards the compound. She passed men moving through the bodies, gravitating towards voices raised in pain, checking the still forms they passed for signs of life. The enemy attackers lying on the ground were dispatched quickly with knives, but she turned her face away so as not to see it.

She'd never been so glad to be royal and not a part of the aftermath of battle. When she reached the compound, she left her horse with one of the servants and asked for water to wash off the worst of the blood striping her limbs. Before it was brought, she fell face down on her sleeping mat, still stinking of battle, and went to sleep.

♦♦♦

When someone touched her shoulder, she sprang to her feet, reaching for her knife before she fully woke up. Seeing Amadou's face, she relaxed. He carried a lit taper in one hand and a bowl with a dark-colored stew in the other. The smell made her mouth water, and she grabbed it from him before he could even attempt to hand it to her.

He sat down on the floor next to her and waited as she ate. Finally, when the bowl was licked clean, he spoke.

"That is just the beginning," he said.

The food in her stomach became a stone, and she had to swallow quickly. "Is it?"

Amadou nodded. His face was tired, and she wondered if he had gotten any rest at all. She couldn't guess what time of night it was. "More Minké outriders were spotted near dusk. They've formed camp in a wide perimeter. The King would like to speak with you when you're ready."

She glanced down at her body, still covered in blood and dust. Behind Amadou, she glimpsed a bowl of water on the floor. "Give me a moment, and I will be."

♦♦♦

"Attack before sunup," her father said.

There were lines across his face that hadn't been there this morning. He looked like he hadn't gotten any rest either—she wondered, suddenly, if she had been the only one. If they had let her sleep because she was the princess. Somehow, the thought didn't sit too comfortably on her

"We'll sleep in shifts. Keep your weapons by your side and

do not stray from the compound. We have rumors about what the Minké do to wandering tribesmen." His voice was grim. Gueri realized she had never seen her father like this, never heard him like this, not even when the two of them had argued before.

She offered to take the next watch. After a long look into her eyes, her father nodded.

Battle the next day was much like the first, but they managed to hold. In the end, more of the Minké warriors were on the ground and fewer of their people. After a week of fighting, the remaining Minké moved on.

"Not the last of them, I bet," said Amadou.

And he was right. Over the next two years, waves of the tribesmen came through, usually aggressive, sometimes not. Once in a while, smaller tribes would be welcomed, marrying into their community. Before long, there were more babies underfoot than one knew what to do with.

Smiling, Amadou told her, "The next generation of warriors."

Gueri went back to her father.

"No!" he told her again.

"Then I will leave here and find someone to marry!" she said.

Her father grabbed her arm. She was strong enough to resist, but she let him march her back to the compound. Silently, the townspeople watched their King lead his horse by one hand, daughter by the other, until they were back within their home. A servant took his mount, but he walked her all the way to her room and put her into it.

"There will be no more argument," he told her and shut the door behind him. She heard a thunk on the other side and stood staring at it for one moment. Then she moved forward, as if in a dream, and pushed against the door.

It was barred from without. She had finally pushed him too far.

♦♦♦

In the middle of the night, she heard something and sat up abruptly from her mat. It was a scraping sound from outside her room. Against the blackness of night, a lighter-colored rectangle appeared—the door, opening. Then blackness reappeared.

Light flared, and she threw up her hands to block her eyes. After blinking several times, she dropped them to see the familiar figure of Amadou. He held a taper in one hand and a bundle under the other arm.

"Quickly," he said. "We don't have much time."

He walked across the room to her and dropped the bundle on her mat. She unrolled it and discovered a hooded peasant tunic and drawstring pants wrapped around a cloth that contained food and drink.

"Hurry. Bring your armor and weapons, but do not wear them. Wrap your mat around them to hide them."

She looked up at Amadou for one moment, seeing not a guard or her friend, but a stranger. "Why?" she asked.

At that, he glanced away, back at the door. "I had a daughter once," he said. "Before you were born."

She nodded and got dressed.

♦♦♦

It couldn't be her own horse they took—he was too easily recognizable, and if he were missing from the stables, it would be that much faster to discovery and pursuit. Instead, Amadou had secured two dun-colored mounts of middle years—not too sleek or too fast, but able to blend into the landscape. "Two?" she asked when she saw them.

He nodded. "I am charged by my King to protect you," he said.

"The King knows I'm leaving?" she asked, startled. But he shook his head. He did not say more.

The sentries saw Amadou and his hooded companion and waved them by. There hadn't been any Minké attacks in nearly half a year. It seemed whatever had caused the tribes to migrate had ended—some of the people who came to them spoke of massive droughts, fields burning, and children dying. But with this winter, there had been plentiful rainfall, more than they had seen in years. The river was full again, as never before.

They moved north, deeper into the savannah, following the river. The Minké came from the eastern branch of the river, so Amadou figured they would be safe heading north.

"Up here, the lands become empty except for wild things," he said one night over their campfire. The food they'd brought had run out, and they were roasting small game brought down with Gueri's arrows. Yesterday had been hare, today a brace of hyrax. They didn't speak about the future or what plans extended beyond surviving each day; Gueri was afraid to think about it. If nothing was out here but animals, where did that leave her?

Her sleep that night was troubled, and she woke the next morning with heavy eyes. They kept their mounts to a walk all that day, and she found herself dozing off at the gentle pace. Amadou seemed no better—once a while, she would glance over and see his head nodding. So it was no surprise that the wandering band of Minké were able to catch them completely unprepared.

The first she knew of them was when her beast whinnied and broke into a run. It was all she could do to hold on as she was snapped out of her half-slumber. She grabbed at the reins, sawing them to slow down her mount, but it was no use. Looking back, she saw that an arrow had pierced the animal near its flank; although the wound was not deep, it was enough to set the horse mad. Glancing farther back, she saw a sight to pierce her heart like an arrow; the Minké were not giving chase to her, but had surrounded Amadou. One rode up to him, and with a swift stab of his arm, ran his spear right through him. Only then did they give chase to her.

Gueri cried out as she saw Amadou fall from his beast, which was rearing against the men holding it. Tears pricked her eyes, but she turned her face forward just in time to guide her mount around a series of low boulders. Her horse was getting less panicked, or perhaps just tiring—either way, the Minké pursing her had already fallen behind and were rapidly losing ground, even though her mount had slowed. She let the animal have its head and kept on riding until her horse finally stumbled to a halt, sides heaving.

The Minké were nowhere in sight. She slithered from her horse's back and rested her face against its side as, finally, she allowed herself to cry.

♦♦♦

The days blurred together after that. Gueri would stop before dark and light a fire to cook her meals, but douse it before true nightfall so as not to show a beacon to those who might follow. She continued to trail the river for lack of a better plan, but her days were miserable, her nights more so. She woke at each rustle in the grass, each call of a night predator, and spent hours staring up at the stars, thinking about home. If she had just been less foolish, more accepting of her father's decrees—if she only had not argued, she would be back home right now. Amadou would be alive. Her teacher, her friend, her companion since childhood, would not be feeding the jackals this night. He would be home with her.

She cried. She didn't know she had so many tears inside of her until now. But after a while had passed, after days by herself in the savannah with no companion except her horse, she longed to turn around and head back. She wished she could apologize to her father, could go home to be welcomed back by her people with open arms. She realized anew just what crime she had committed in fleeing, how she had turned her back on her responsibilities.

If the Minké who had attacked them weren't still out there, weren't still behind her, she would have gone back. But she couldn't be sure, and in her mind's eye, she saw the impact of the spear through Amadou's gut, saw the slow fall from his horse. She didn't want to die out here, alone and unmourned, and so she could not turn back.

The next day, the river curved to the east. She stopped at the bend, shading her eyes against the sun. Across the river, there were many trees banded together. She could find shelter and cover under them, perhaps even head west and then double back south. Perhaps she could really go home.

But if she followed the bend of the river—that would lead to Minké territory. Perhaps she was too far north to run into more of them, but perhaps not. She dismounted and allowed her animal to graze as she deliberated. The sun was high overhead by the time she climbed back into her saddle and guided her horse into the river.

The horse didn't like it. The river was slow-moving, but rivers were not without peril. Much farther down the banks, she saw what looked like logs on shore—logs that slipped, one by one, into the river. She urged her mount to swim faster. The river wasn't wide, but crocodiles were fast swimmers.

Just when she thought there was no hope, her beast gave a massive heave of its legs and they clopped out of the water. Behind them, the water churned, and she urged her horse away from the bank at a brisk trot.

Under the trees, it was cooler. She heard a loud chittering sound—monkeys, by the sound of them, but she never saw any of them. As they progressed through the trees, the trunks grew closer and closer together, and the branches stretched taller and taller; before she knew it, the light from the sun had turned green, and they were in a deep forest.

She had never been in such a place. The chittering was louder now, and as she looked up, she began to catch glimpses of movement. Just a flash here and there, never anything more, never something distinct enough to tell what it was. Unease crept up her spine, and the coolness made her shiver. Long before nightfall, she had tethered her horse and gathered enough deadfall to start a fire. She kept it burning throughout the long night, waking to strange sounds and adding more branches whenever roused.

"Well, now I'm lost," she told her horse the next day once

seated on its back again. The sun didn't show through the branches at all. Her plan to swing west was less ideal without a west to find. She chose a direction at random and continued on.

Although still strange, Gueri was growing used to the noises of the forest. The chittering had stopped bothering her, although the strange creaking and sway of branches sometimes did, for it sounded as if something large and heavy were passing overhead. She still caught glimpses of movement, but as long as she remained mounted on her horse or seated by a fire at night, nothing seemed to want to bother her by coming closer. More than ever, she longed for Amadou, who she was sure would have been able to tell her about this forest. When he was young, he had traveled far and wide, met many different tribes and knew the land for miles around. While he had told her some of the stories from his youth, she had listened indifferently, as only the young can do. Now, she wished she could recall more than the thought that some menace stalked her, some danger that she could not name.

That night, she fed branches into the fire until it blazed. She caught a strange animal she had never seen before—it had large ears and a bloated belly—but when she skinned and cooked it, it tasted like hyrax. Maybe it was a forest variety.

She fell asleep with a full belly and woke to the sense of danger. She opened her eyes to slits and saw that across the fire from her, a man was sitting watching her. He wore leggings but no shirt, and his chest was covered with lighter, tan markings that stood out sharply against his dark skin.

He didn't appear to be doing anything other than watching her, and so she chose to open her eyes fully and rose to one elbow. When he didn't speak, she said, "Hello."

The man smiled. His teeth were very white, his expression friendly. "I wondered if you were a forest sprite," he said. "But I didn't think one would have a nomad's horse."

His laughter was light and made her want to smile. She levered herself up so that she was sitting, mirroring his cross-legged pose.

"No sprite," she answered easily. "Just a traveler." She always slept with her weapons at hand, but as she discreetly flicked her eyes to the side, she saw that they had been moved. They weren't right next to the man, either, but he had placed them some distance away from both of them, next to her mount.

It relaxed her somewhat. If he had intended to kill her, she had given him ample opportunity while sleeping. Same if he intended to steal her belongings. No, it seemed he was merely curious, as he had said.

"And where are you traveling from?"

She shrugged, glancing around. It was still night, and the glare of the campfire illuminated a circle around them through the trees. She could see little, though.

"From a kingdom in the south," she finally answered. "And where are you from?"

He leapt to his feet, and she made an aborted grab for her knife before she realized he was holding out his hand to her. Tentatively, she placed her hand out to be gripped by his; a warrior's greeting. "Names first," he said. "I am Riale."

"Gueri," she said after a deliberate pause, as she wondered whether to give her full name or not. She chose no, simply because her fame had traveled far and wide among the local tribes. She didn't know if they were far enough away that he would have heard of her, but she didn't want to take the chance.

"A pretty name," he replied, his hand lingering on hers. His eyes glinted. Then he released her hand and sat back down. She had come to her knees when grabbing for her knife, and so she settled back also. "I am an elephant hunter, but lost the spoor that I was tracking when I came across you. My people live in the north, but we travel with the game. Lately, there have been others coming through here that are . . . well, they are not so friendly." He looked out at the dark much as she had, but she didn't think he saw the night. Instead, he seemed lost in a memory that was not pleasant.

"Yes," she replied softly. He glanced back at her, saw the pain that was twisting her features. Unbidden, her eyes grew watery and she swiped at her cheeks. "The Minké. We have been plagued by them also. They killed my companion on the savannah, and I have been traveling since then to escape them."

"Escape?" He leapt to his feet again, alert. "Are they close behind you?" He started to kick dirt on the fire.

She held out a hand to stop him. "No, no. I don't know where they are. That was days ago. I ran from them, and kept going north. Then I came to the bend in the river and continued through this forest—but, I must admit I am lost."

This time, his smile was brighter than the fire. "I would consider it my honor," he said, bowing low, "if you would allow me to help you find your way."

She laughed for the first time in days at the absurdly courtly gesture. She hadn't seen anything closely resembling his behavior since she left home. "And I would be honored," she said, "to accept your help."

♦♦♦

He had no horse, but he was much taller than her, and his stride matched her horse's trot. Under the trees, however, they didn't make good time as they picked their way over and around the tangled growth. "You are lucky," he said as they made camp the next night. "There are many creatures here that do not welcome humans." When asked, he would not name them. "To name them is to summon them," is all he would say.

Gueri had never met someone like him. He always had a ready smile for her and gently teased her whenever he could. She found herself laughing more often than not, eager to learn about his life. Each night, they murmured quietly together long past when they should be asleep, and she knew he was as reluctant to end the conversation as she.

They came out of the forest on the fifth day—Riale had assured her they were headed west and would then turn south when they reached the savannah. "How far south?" he asked her, but she just shook her head. She couldn't remember the number of days.

That night as they spoke side by side, something changed. She could tell by the way he was looking at her, his eyes intense as a lion's. Slowly, as if fearing she would run, he reached out a hand and cupped her cheek.

"You are beautiful," he said.

She had heard such words before. But she had never *felt* them, felt as if they were being spoken just to her. He leaned closer to her, hesitating when his breath touched her lips. A second later, he kissed her.

Gueri's heart pounded. Riale was handsome and friendly and funny, and she had never met anyone like him.

That night, they let the fire burn down to embers, intent on other things. And the next day, she walked beside him, leading her horse behind her.

♦♦♦

Time passed much more quickly than when she rode north by herself, grieving for lost Amadou. They were not attacked by the Minké, although they spotted roaming bands of them on more than one occasion, but were able to avoid confrontation hiding in the tall grasses. Gueri did not count the days, caught up in a happiness that seemed eternal. Although it was weeks, it could have been only moments later that they spotted the walls of the compound in the distance.

She heard Riale's sharp intake of breath. "You are Moga?" he asked her sharply.

Gueri turned to him, suddenly afraid what she would see on his face. But she saw nothing but wonder.

"I have heard of the Moga Kingdom," he said, meeting her eyes. She saw the beginnings of understanding in them, and it twisted in her heart. "Ruled by a King . . . and his warrior daughter."

Dropping her gaze, she nodded. But he tapped a finger against her chin, which made her look up again. He was smiling.

"What is there to fear?" he asked. "Let us meet this fierce warrior princess, then." He laughed, which set her to laughing, too.

And so, laughing, they walked the final distance to the compound. Hand in hand, united, they walked through the gates of her home to greet her father and her people once again.

She hadn't expected a hero's welcome—she had crept out in the night like a traitor. But what she got was unnerving.

People stared. Men and women, children, warriors, the young and the old. Whatever they were doing—baking bread, beating mats, scouring pots, weaving cloth—everything ceased, as if time fled before the soft advance of Gueri's feet.

Her hand shook. Riale gripped it tightly, almost hard enough to hurt, and the shaking was hidden.

The guards unfroze long enough to let them into the compound. One took her horse, another her spear. Servants bowed and stepped aside as she paced down the dim corridors and into the receiving hall.

Finally, there was the familiar figure standing in front of her, a cloak of courtiers spread out behind him. His heavy-lidded eyes gave away nothing. The King waited, but her dry mouth was empty of words.

Riale was an elephant hunter, and large beasts, animal or human, caused no fear in him. He bowed and said simply, "Your Majesty, I have traveled many days with your daughter. I would ask for your blessing on our marriage."

The King did not look surprised. In fact, no expression crossed his features when he turned from Riale to his daughter. "Princess Guerrière," he said, his voice stern. "I forbade you to marry, yet you return here with this man. What have you to say?"

Gueri turned to the man at her side—tall, gentle, and with humor written in the lines etched around his smiling mouth. Riale had experienced war, as she had. He had survived. But he'd looked beyond battle and found her.

She turned back to the King. His cheeks were thin, and his

mouth pulled down.

"Father," she said. "Fighting is my gift. I have used it to stop the Minké when they attacked. Do you think the gods made me a fighter so I will stop now, even if it means fighting against the King?" She tried to smile.

"You are married," her father said abruptly. "I will accept it." He strode out of the room and did not look back.

It was the last time they spoke. One week later, a new wave of Minké came, and the King died with a spear through the neck. When they buried him, Riale held her hand tightly to hide her shaking.

"Long live Queen Guerrière!" he was the first to shout. Then the rest of the tribe took up the chant.

She had no tears for her father, as she had for Amadou. It was war, and sometimes his decisions had cost lives. Including his own.

Yet he had also saved lives. More than that, if he hadn't forbidden her to marry, she never would have left. And out of Amadou's death, she had met Riale.

Out of her father's death, she could save the kingdom. She knew about the heart of war, and what it would take to protect her people from the Minké. There were many more miles to walk on this path.

Gueri turned to Riale. He looked down at her and smiled.

For the first time, she no longer resented the journey.

♦ ♦ A FARMER'S GOOD LUCK ♦ ♦

THE BEST TIME TO CUT bamboo was at the end of the rainy season and the beginning of the dry season. Cut too early and it would be moist and crack later on during the dry season—houses collapsed when bamboo was cut too early. Cut too late and it would be sweet as sugar and attract insects to eat it, causing many problems for the people living there. It was Take's job to determine the best season and work quickly for a good harvest. The best bamboo came from this time, and he could sell it for the highest price.

So it was nearing the end of summer when he was walking through the stand, assessing the stalks. There was a brief break in the rain; the air felt cooler as it became drier. Under the stalks, it was dark already, although out in a field, the sky still held the violet of sunset. He moved by feel and the change in the air and was lulled by the music of the plants, the loud shushing of the leaves. His eyes were useless in the dark, so he closed them and walked forward using his hands and the hardened soles of his feet, knowing the land better than he knew his own body.

Suddenly, his eyelids glowed red and he opened them to see the stalks of bamboo outlined by a powerful light, a glow so bright that he had to hold his hand before his face. He couldn't see the source of the light, but it was blocking his path home. He'd seen wildfire before, but this brightness was too strong to be flames and did not carry their heat.

He walked forward through the stalks with his heart racing in his throat. Tales of spirits filled his head, and he wondered what torment he would suffer at their hands. He knew the old tales, and a simple bamboo farmer like him, living by the plenty of the seasons, had nothing worthy to offer them. He couldn't give fine wines or meat, couldn't even offer a child of his body, for he and his wife had never had any. They were poor in all things but love.

Squinting through the shifting stalks, he finally came to the source of the brilliance. He bent down, unable to see clearly, and felt around with his calloused hands. It felt like just another stalk of bamboo, only swollen close to the ground with some hideous growth. He brought out his knife, picturing all the days of his life, wondering if this was the end for him. As he cut into the tough stalk, he closed his eyes against the glare and held out his hands.

A weight fell against his palms and his eyelids became black. The light had been snuffed with the final slash of the knife. He opened his eyes, but was blinded by the sudden darkness and couldn't see what he held.

♦♦♦

Tsuma stood in the doorway waiting for Take. It was unlike him to be out much beyond twilight, and dinner was waiting on the table. She fanned her face in the heat, waving away the black flies.

When she finally saw movement, she knew it was him. They had been married too long for her to mistake her husband for a stranger, but she saw that he was carrying something. The light from behind her was too dim to tell what it was.

And then she heard it. The sound she had always longed to hear, but never expected to welcome to her home: a baby crying. The light fell on Take's face like a benediction and she saw the tracks of tears down his cheeks.

"We will call her Kaguya-hime," he said. "Our bamboo princess. Our daughter."

♦♦♦

The couple was not young. As if understanding that, the little girl proved easy to care for. She slept the whole night through and ate the pottage Tsuma made in the morning. She did not cry at all other than that first aborted wail when brought before the light of their cottage. And her cry then had been musical and low, like the natural shush of bamboo leaves.

Take told Tsuma the story of how he had found the baby. Tsuma believed the tale unquestioned, for the child could not be a natural creature. She was too beautiful, too perfect, to be born of an earthly mother and father. And her eyes shone with a glow like the moon's, soft and radiant.

The next morning, Tsuma strapped Kaguya to her back to take her into the fields. She was quietly working nearby to Take, Kaguya sleeping on her back, when she heard her husband scream in the next stand of bamboo. *Here is the cost for my perfect daughter*, she thought and went running over to him. Her mind swirled with thoughts of a severed hand or leg, cut through by the sharp machetes they used to harvest the bamboo. Instead, she found Take sitting flat-out on the ground, staring at his two still-attached hands. She looked for blood, but there was nothing. "What? What is it?"

His palms were cupped around something and he raised it up to her, wordless. In the center of his hands was a small nugget of gold.

"Where?" she whispered.

"In the center of the stalk," he said, and she saw his dropped machete behind him and the fallen swathes of bamboo. Inside each stalk was a golden heart.

She laughed, which woke Kaguya, and the baby laughed too. Take stood up and hugged her, hard. Then he pulled the baby from the sling and spun her round and round while the child laughed and laughed.

"You are our wonderful princess! We should have called you good-luck instead," he told her.

♦♦♦

They ate meat with every meal now, and built a grand house next to the bamboo fields. Kaguya grew up, as children do, and she became lovelier with each passing year. Take became known far and wide as a humble man with a generous heart, and he entertained visitors from all walks of life, who took with them tales of the old farmer with the beautiful daughter.

On Kaguya's sixteenth birthday, a horseman arrived bearing a sealed message. Take held it in his hands when given it, but looked helplessly up at the man in brightly lacquered armor perched far above him. "I cannot read," Take told the man, who sneered and snatched back the missive.

"The Emperor Mikado has heard of the beauty of Kaguya-hime. He will be here tomorrow at daybreak."

Take grew pale. Tsuma burst into tears. Kaguya, herself, looked peaceful and serene. Then again, she had always been unnaturally calm, even when very young.

The village turned themselves inside out to help the family prepare for the Emperor's visit. Red banners lined the houses. Children were washed and threatened with dire punishments if they got dirty again. Take bit his nails down to the quick, and Tsuma shut herself in their bedroom and didn't come out until the evening meal. Her eyes were swollen and red, as if she had been crying the entire day. Only Kaguya ate each grain of rice with gentle precision, her face expressionless. She seemed to not know the importance of the Emperor's visit, or not care.

Take and Tsuma did not sleep that night. When the sky first brightened, they stared into each other's eyes. They had been together for a long time, and had been old even when Kaguya had come to them. Now, they were older still, and the same fear was in their hearts. But they said nothing to each other, at least no words aloud.

Take's bones creaked. Tsuma's back ached. They rose and threw open their doors as the sun crested the hills and shone like a funeral lamp upon their home.

Lines of soldiers trotted up the path on matched horses. There were too many for the narrow path that led from the village, and their horses milled nervously in the small space. Their ranks parted around the house and a man dressed in golden robes came walking up the dirt path, his litter too wide to be carried this far. He was neither young nor old, handsome or ugly. And he did not smile.

Take and Tsuma dropped painfully to their knees and bowed their heads before the man. So they did not see Kaguya step out the door from behind them, nor did they see the Emperor's face when he saw their daughter. If Take had seen their visitor's face at that moment, he might have recognized the expression of a man who had fallen hopelessly in love. Or perhaps he wouldn't have, since he'd never seen his own face upon seeing Tsuma for the first time, those many decades before.

Tsuma, however, glanced up at Kaguya's face as her daughter first looked at the Emperor. And she saw nothing in her daughter's face. No expression, no greeting or recognition. Absolutely nothing at all.

♦♦♦

After his knees failed him and Tsuma helped him stand, Take invited the Emperor into his home and served him the best dishes, prepared by his wife with her own hands. The Emperor ate little, merely stared across the table at Kaguya. At the end of the meal, the man said, "Marry me."

"No, thank you," their daughter replied calmly. Bowing, she left the room.

The next day, the Emperor arrived with a fanfare and a chest full of glowing emeralds, strings of perfectly matched white and black pearls, and silver crowns studded with rubies. "Marry me," he told their daughter and, "No," she replied.

The days passed, and with each one the Emperor brought a new gift and the same request. However, Kaguya's answer never varied and the spring season pressed closer to summer. On the solstice would be the full moon.

Each month since her daughter's thirteenth birthday, Tsuma had noticed Kaguya grow restless on the night of the full moon. The girl would sit outside for hours, no matter the weather, and stare up into the sky. Even when there were clouds or the worst storms, she would disappear outdoors and not reappear until the moon had reached its zenith. Then she would return to the house, her glowing eyes dimmed, and take to her bed without a word.

This night was no exception. However, this time Tsuma followed her daughter out of doors and watched her. She was worried enough about the Emperor's proximity to wonder if he would dare kidnap the girl on a night such as tonight. But she didn't expect to find what she saw.

The moon glowed down from a serene sky. And Kaguya, looking up, wore the expression of a woman very much in love.

"What is it?" Tsuma asked, her old voice creaking with the weight of her years. She knew, even then, without asking. She felt it in her bones.

Kaguya looked at the woman who had raised her, at the only mother she'd ever known. And she answered, as calmly as she ever had. "My home. They are coming for me. Soon, they will be here."

♦♦♦

Unlike the moon, the Emperor's love and patience didn't wane over the next month. He might never have realized a change was coming except that Tsuma became ill. She dared say nothing to Take, afraid his heart would break as hers was breaking under the burden of her new knowledge. Kaguya would have stayed at her bedside and nursed her, but the pain of her daughter's presence made Tsuma's health deteriorate. Finally, she sent her daughter away from her, too heartsick to care.

The Emperor visited the old woman in her bed. "What is it?" he asked her, but she turned her face from him. He was afraid of what he saw in her eyes. And so he set guards around their house night and day, leaving Kaguya and her family trapped within.

The days passed, but Tsuma knew when the time had come of the full moon, because Kaguya disregarded her edict and came to visit her. The girl took her foster mother's frail hand in hers, and her beauty was so overwhelming in its intensity that Tsuma had to close her eyes.

"I love you, Mama," she said in her musical voice. "I will always love you. But I do not belong here anymore." She kissed the old woman on the cheek, and Tsuma opened her eyes to watch her daughter walk away from her. Then the old woman turned her face to the wall.

Kaguya came upon Take, who was crying silently where he stood by the door. He put his arms around her, but there seemed nothing to grasp—she felt as light as air. "I love you,

Papa," she said. He let go of her and she opened the door and walked into the night.

Three figures waited for her. They glowed so brightly that they blinded the human eyes of the Emperor's guards. When the light of their presence faded, Kaguya was gone, too.

Take joined Tsuma in their bed, and they held each other close as the night passed into day. They did not rise again from their bed, and when the Emperor discovered them both gone from this earth the next morning, as if to escape his wrath by joining their daughter, he stared at their bodies for a long, long time, seeming to age and harden as the moments passed. When he finally walked away, he ordered his guards to set fire to the house and salt the fields. When the fire cleared and the embers settled, nothing grew there, from that day until today.

Emperor Mikado returned to his capital city and didn't set foot in Dewa Province for the rest of his life. But on his deathbed, he was said to look up at the moon and murmur a name. And the look in his eyes was one of love.

♦ ♦ ♦ IN DUE RESCUE ♦ ♦ ♦

IT WOULD BE A TERRIBLE cliché to say Princess Filomena couldn't believe her eyes. But, to be honest, if she had imagined a knight rescuing her today, it would have been someone like Sir Galahad or Sir Lancelot—strong, noble, and shiny—riding up on a blinding white charger that had more frills and pennants than a tournament.

Not this guy. His armor was piecemeal, splattered with mud, and his helmet looked like the visor had rusted in a halfway-up, halfway-down position. A twig would have called him skinny. Even the man's horse wasn't quite white, but more of an assorted and uncomplementary beige.

"Either I'm no longer the favorite—and I must be, because I'm the only heir—or the standards have gone down since I was first kidnapped." She crossed her arms and tapped her foot on the hard surface of the well-traveled dirt road.

The man attempted to raise the visor of his helmet with one gauntleted hand. There was quite an assault on her eardrums as metal scraped metal, but no obvious progress. Finally, he gave up, took the entire thing off, and hooked it precariously on the pommel of his swaybacked mount. "I have come to rescue you, oh fair Princess Filomena Rosita Bonita Bobanee Bonanafanna Fofannee—"

"Just call me Fil," the princess interrupted, waving away the twenty or so names that were attached to her in formal surroundings. "Look, there's no time for all that. What's your plan?"

"Plan?" The knight scratched his head. "Well, go to the witch's castle where the princess—erm, you—are being held captive—"

Fil jerked a thumb over her shoulder. "It's that way."

"Erm—and creep in at night—"

Fil looked around at the bright, sunny morning. "You'd have a bit of a wait."

"And, erm, then untie you from your bonds—"

Fil held up her unmarked wrists. "The witch never tied me up. Classic mistake to underestimate a princess's ability to walk out a door. But do go on."

"And then throw you over my shoulder—"

Fil couldn't help it. She snorted with laughter at that. "And after you fell down, then what?"

The man was getting a bit red in the face. "Well, then, take you home to your father, of course. And ask for your hand in marriage."

"Look, Sir… well, I never got your name. Who are you?"

"Sir Ahibishekilama the Fourth."

The princess shook her head. "I can't pronounce that! I'll call you Sir Ah. Okay, Sir Ah, you're welcome to carry on with your plan. In the meantime, I think I'll just walk back home."

"Oh, no!" For the first time, Sir Ah seemed to recall who he was talking to. He slid off his horse in a rattle of metal plates. It turned out, once he was on the ground, he didn't look so gangly anymore. It was just his long limbs and thinness that made him look like a skeleton perched atop a nag headed for the stew pot. "I must insist. Please, mount my noble steed and let me guide you back to your castle."

At this, Fil snorted again. "I don't know if I would care to mount anything of yours. And certainly not your 'noble steed.' Nah, you take him. I've got legs. I'll walk."

After ten minutes spent arguing about the propriety of letting the princess preamble versus Fil's equally adamant derision of his hack, Fil finally just rolled her eyes and strode off. Behind her, she could hear Sir Ah rattling his way back aboard his horse and kicking it in an attempt to catch up to her long stride.

After several moments of silence (or, as close as one could come with an unhappy horse trotting along, bearing a man wearing an ill-fitting assortment of armor), Fil sighed. "I *suppose* if you aren't too annoying, I might let you take credit for the rescue. It was, after all, very nice of you to come all this way."

Sir Ah, whose head had been hanging so low from dejection that it looked like it would fall off, perked right up. "Oh, would you? That would be grand!"

"But none of this marriage business," Fil scowled. "I already have a plan, and it doesn't involve an obligatory marriage to the first—or fiftieth—idiot who comes along thinking I'm an easy way to the throne." As Sir Ah's expression started to fall again, she added, "No offense."

"So what is your plan?"

"Right now, our kingdom is run along a feudal system, which is a very inexact form of financing, especially in times of peace. I think we need to create a dialogue across class lines of noble obligation which is less noblesse oblige, and more pounds and pence. It's a language everyone speaks."

"I . . . see." Sir Ah scratched his head, his helmet still balanced on the saddle in front of him. "But what does that mean in practical terms?"

"Revolutionizing our taxation system. Incentives, deductions, a plan with more foresight than 'soak them for everything they've got.' It's all quite complicated." Fil waved a hand airily. "I have the documents drawn up. All it needs is the king's signature. If enough of the nobles get behind this, we can create a brand-new society here."

"Tax laws." Sir Ah's eyes seemed a bit glazed. "A revolution of taxes?"

"Better than the other kind of revolution, with everyone stabbing pointy things at each other." Fil winked at Sir Ah in an attempt at conspiracy, but he didn't seem to notice her awkward flirtation. Oh, well. "Are we in agreement, then?"

Sir Ah focused back on the princess. "In agreement about what?"

"You take credit for the rescue. In return, you back my tax reform bill. It's all quite simple, really." Fil sighed. It was hard to get through the man's thick skull. The last ten knights who had "rescued" her had been a lot quicker on the uptake. Still, she couldn't ignore any landholder. She needed a majority to sway her father, whose eyes tended to glaze over like Sir Ah's whenever she brought up the reforms she sought to implement.

"Oh." Sir Ah cleared his throat. "Yes, yes. Of course. I'd be honored." He attempted to make a half-bow from his saddle, but his helmet, precariously perched, was jostled at the gesture. It dropped to the ground with a thud and rolled over to the princess.

Sighing again, she picked up the battered helmet and handed it back. "Every vote counts," she muttered to herself. Then, louder, "Okay, let's hoof it, shall we? I'm on a tight schedule."

Her friend, the "witch," would be expecting her back tomorrow morning. Just in time for "rescue" by another clueless knight on their shortening list—nobles who hadn't found out the real reason behind the princess's regular absences from court.

The king would roll his eyes, clandestinely summon the next name on her list, and the process would start all over again. Her father's motivation to go along with her "crazy" scheme was to marry her off, she knew. But little did he know that she only had a few votes to go to put her plan into action.

Although, the next time around, Fil hoped for someone more like Sir Galahad. A strong and practiced warrior who would gallantly battle dragons to rescue her.

Or, if she was being terribly prosaic . . . at least a knight who could carry on a decent conversation for the walk back home.

♦ ♦ THE SOLDIER'S CHOICE ♦ ♦

IF THERE WAS ONE MAN whom Shazia could call a friend, it was Ibin.

Most people thought that he should have followed in his father's footsteps and become a warrior rather than a . . . well, whatever he was. When she'd first come to Castle Var, she'd thought the same thing when she'd heard rumors about Rabanar's useless second son.

"A layabout," the maid had told her, buckling together the sides of Shazia's leather armor before the banquet dinner. Shazia had dressed herself since she was old enough to walk, but she wasn't about to argue with a woman who could have hidden a small pony under her skirts. "Just be sure to talk to Pelligor seated on your left—he's a decent sort of man, with a son who's just beginning his training." The woman eyed her charge critically. "You're pretty big for your age, aren't you? Suck in a bit, I need to tighten these straps."

The chair on her right was empty when she was escorted to her seat moments later, trying to remember how to breathe in armor that, with the maid's help, was as restrictive as a corset. It wasn't until the first and second course had been served and taken away that the tramp of heavy boots interrupted the quiet conversation flowing through the hall.

"Sorry, sorry," a voice announced loudly behind her as the man reached the vacant chair. "My valet must have gotten the time wrong . . . again." Up and down the table, small chuckles escaped as, with a flourish, the man pulled back the seat and settled himself comfortably before clapping his hands in a foppish manner. Servants rushed up with the third course before Ibin could cause another disturbance.

Without looking around at his other dining companions, the young man turned to face her. "They must have warned you about me, I expect," he said. "I am a poet, a dreamer, and a mischief-maker, no more. No matter what has been said. How may I entertain my lady?"

It was the first time she'd laughed in a month, ever since she'd first learned she was to begin her training at Castle Var.

From that moment on, the unlikely couple had been friends. Ibin justified it as, "I've been forced to keep you company because it keeps me out of trouble."

Often, the opposite was true—he seemed to help get her *into* trouble. Or, at the very least, to get her into awkward situations which could have turned into trouble if he hadn't also had a flair for defusing those same situations. As her training progressed, she would either turn to him in frustration for his lackadaisical attitude—didn't he take anything seriously?—or in envy. He lived the lifestyle she had turned her back on, and she sometimes wished for a life of luxury, especially when she was covered in fresh bruises after learning a new maneuver on the field.

On her fifteenth birthday, she was surprised to be turned away at the training yard. "Orders are from Rabanar. He's entertaining visitors from the south today." The guard captain shrugged noncommittally. "A groom's waiting at the stables for you."

The "groom" standing in the stable yards turned out to be a laughing Ibin. "Don't worry, I didn't forge my father's note," he'd admitted when she didn't join in the laughter. "He really does have business today. But you, young miss," ignoring her glower, "are now entering adulthood. Since no family member has stepped forward to coach you at this crucial step in life, I have volunteered to sacrifice myself in this duty for the greater good." He thumped his chest dramatically with one fist, then extravagantly waved to an imaginary cheering crowd. "Yes, the self-sacrifice, the burden of such a great duty . . ."

"Oh, hush," she finally laughed. "You'll scare the real grooms from their duty with such talk." Ibin had been waiting with two saddled horses—the sturdy brown gelding that was "hers" during training and his favorite mare, a dainty side-stepper with a blue-gray coat. She grabbed the reins of her mount from his slack hand and whipped them around the horse's neck as she leapt onto its back. "Are you going to stand there all day?"

"You . . ." he muttered as he gained his own mount's back. "Race you to the front gate!" he shouted, already kneeing his horse forward. She grinned as she gave her beast its head. They raced, neck and neck, down the path from the stable yards, through the fields where men and women paused in their labors, straightened their backs, and raised hands against the glare of the sun to watch the two young people at play. The grain was ripening nearby; the far fields, away from the main road, were reserved for vineyards. Over the undulating hills of yellow, she could see the blue-green dots of the vines in carefully tended rows stretching towards the nearby mountains.

The stone posts of the gate marking the entrance to Rabanar's lands were just on the far side of the next hill. Shazia's gelding was no foal, but it was a much sturdier beast than Ibin's younger, more delicate mare. By the time Shazia slowed at the stone markings, the white mare had already decided it had had enough and had slowed down despite Ibin's loud protests and prodding. It sauntered up to the gate and lowered its head to nibble on a sprig of alfalfa growing by the edge of the dirt path.

"That'll teach me to trust this miserable excuse for a fleabag." He slapped the horse's shoulder in mock-anger. The mare shrugged one shoulder and didn't even lift her head. At the motion, both Ibin and Shazia started to laugh.

"Oh, stop, stop," the young girl gasped. "I have bruised ribs from yesterday—this is killing me!"

"Speaking of killing," Ibin said with a wicked grin. "I have a recipe for fun that's sure to kill you." Shazia wiped away moisture from her eyes and nodded, still winded. "As a young male warrior, your fifteenth birthday would be marked with a centuries-old rite of passage." At her raised eyebrows, he specified, "We'd buy you a whore and a barrel of wine." Shazia's jaw dropped. Ibin cleared his throat in the awkward silence. "Yes, well, that seems inappropriate at this time. So does the rite of passage for a young woman—celebrating your betrothal to some stuffy lord you've never met. So I figured I'd split the difference."

"You're going to buy me a whore and betroth me to her?" Shazia asked innocently.

The shocked silence was broken by his loud laughter. A pair of offended crows rose abruptly from the nearby field and cawed as they settled down again.

"Not exactly the direction I was going, but I'll keep it in mind," he chuckled. "As a warrior, you do need to know how to drink. So I figured I would introduce you to the world of army alcohol—namely, the vilest liquor known to humankind. After that, I have a special surprise for you." He jerked at the reins of his horse and got the lazy white mare moving after a few tugs. He pointed her nose south, towards town. Shazia kneed her mount to follow, and they trotted along the road for several seconds, the dull beats of hooves thudding against the hard-packed earth.

"I don't know if I can survive any more of your surprises," Shazia commented dryly into the silence.

"That's the whole point," he replied mysteriously. "Just wait and see."

♦ ♦ ♦

Shazia blinked, shading her eyes. Ibin had given her a thorough introduction to the finest rotgut in the region, and she wasn't sure if the row of tents in front of them were waving in the breeze or if her vision was waving her, instead.

"I was keeping an eye out for them," Ibin murmured in her ear as she tried to focus on the nearby picture-signs hung in front of each tent. "Peori's traveling band of entertainers.

They're normally through here twice a year, once heading north during the summer and again south in the fall." He grabbed her arm and hustled her past the first few tents, finally stopping at the edge of the cleared area. The last tent stood slightly apart from the others, and it was dyed a deep, dark red. "This is the one." Ibin pushed something into her hand, then shoved her through the tent flap before she could think of anything to say.

Either due to the cooler evening air outside or to the small brazier inside, Shazia immediately felt as if she were choking on the hot air of the interior. A small table covered by a crudely dyed red cloth dominated the center of the tent, and a middle-aged woman, just on the far side of childbearing years, sat opposite the entrance with her colorful skirts spread around her.

Shazia glanced down into her sweaty palm and saw that Ibin had given her a coin—the first she'd ever handled in her life. The gypsy in front of her gestured to the cushion in front of the table and murmured in a surprisingly deep voice, "Please, be seated. I will tell your fortune for a silver."

Numbly, she knelt on the indicated cushion and held out her hand. Either the alcoholic haze or the simple speed of an offered fare made the coin seem to disappear like magic—one moment, it lay heavy in her hand, the next, the gypsy's cool hands covered hers and Shazia's palm was empty.

"Your friend was correct that this is a good place to find a rite of passage," the woman's deep voice intoned. Shazia closed her eyes to stop the spinning of the room, but it only made her stomach lurch, since she had no place to focus her attention other than the sound of the woman's voice. She opened her eyes again, but a closer look at the gypsy's face showed deep lines and a scar across one brow that looked like a knife had inflicted the original wound. Shazia shivered, despite the heat.

A nursery rhyme from her youth—about gypsy women stealing noblemen's children—buzzed in her head, most of the words a forgotten blur. She could almost hear her mother's voice singing it as she fell asleep—her head jerked as her eyes drooped. The gypsy had thrown a handful of some incense on the brazier, and a scented smoke curled from the edges of the coals across the room. Despite the musty odor, the smell seemed to clear the fuzziness around the edges of her mind. She noticed that the gypsy's eyes were a pale gray, like her own. She felt a stab of homesickness and could almost recall the sound of her mother's singing again.

"You've traveled far from your birthplace, but you have farther you must go." The woman touched Shazia's hands lightly, which she'd rested on the reddened cloth. The patterns of the uneven dye job seemed to move in the smoke-filled atmosphere, like something alive and breathing. The woman flung her hand out in a contemptuous wave—in the meantime, her other hand snuck into the long sleeves she wore and pulled out a deck of large, painted cards. Shazia grimaced at the attempted trickery, and her opinion, never high in the face of supposed magic and sorceries, lowered further.

The gypsy gestured and Shazia dropped her hands to her lap. The entertainer passed her hand over the deck three times in a circle, then shuffled it with a choppy flick of her wrist. The first card laid face up was a man holding a sword in one hand and a white dove in the other. "The soldier," the woman intoned, as if the name would hold meaning for Shazia. The next card: "The traveler," she murmured as a man in a ragged cloak with a jewel-headed walking stick looked up at her. As the gypsy pulled out the third card—three being the holy number of Yrdun, patron of warriors—a fourth card fell also, caught against the edge of the third. "Ahhh—" breathed the gypsy. "This means a choice that you must face. On one side—" the card she had pulled was a black-cloaked figure standing on a pile of corpses, "there is death. On the other—" and the caught card showed a picture of an crowned man on a white horse, with each corner of the rectangle engraved with the image of a book, "there are heroic deeds and a name set in legend. Like most choices, you cannot know which action will lead to which result. But the choice will be presented to you after many years have passed, spurred in part by a plot to control your actions. Since the third card is death and the fourth, or unasked-for, card is fame and glory, you must carefully consider the choices you face and not necessarily take the first path shown."

Shazia's stomach gave a burping sound. Swallowing against the thick feeling in her throat, she challenged, "But what does it mean?"

"Ahhh." The woman smiled. Meant to be mysterious, the gypsy only looked sly. "This is your first time seeking a fortune, then, and you are skeptical. What it means is that the hardest choice you must face is in your future. Right now, your path has been laid, and all you must do is follow it to a place you've already decided to go. You have been wondering at your choices so far, but they have been the choices you were meant to make. The gods have given their favor to your actions."

Shazia would have snorted, but was unsure what such an action would do to her precarious hold on her stomach's contents. "Thank you," she mumbled, standing up at a half-crouch. Standing was a mistake, she decided, as she hurriedly pushed aside the tent flap. Five steps more outside and she found a shrub to serve as a convenient location to settle her stomach in a very abrupt and not-too-pleasing way.

Before she was finished, the familiar sound of laughter drowned out the choking sounds she was making. "That bad of a fortune, eh?" Ibin guffawed.

If she had been feeling just the slightest bit better, she would have smacked him across the head for getting her into this situation. As it was, she suffered his help, since there was no way she was getting back to the castle on her own.

Despite feeling the worst she'd ever felt in her life, by the time she was lying prone in bed and close to passing out, she spared one moment to reflect on what the gypsy had told her.

Rubbish, was her last conscious thought.

♦♦♦

When Shazia was young, she would often sneak away from her nursemaid after midday meal to the upper levels of her father's castle.

The south wing of the castle was used only during festivals to house foreign nobles. Most of the year, it stood empty. The inner corridor in the south wing looked out over the training grounds of the warriors.

Shazia would use her stolen time to lean out of the open-air windows to watch the soldiers practicing their craft below. From so far above, the sounds of battle echoed against the walls like ghosts. She would hear random shouted words and the clash of metal on metal in spurts of noise that changed as the wind moved.

One day as she was leaning out the window watching the men practice, Rabanar's voice rang out behind her, causing her to jump and spin to face him. She almost didn't catch herself in time to prevent joining the combatants below in a most unusual manner. He grinned at her.

"Why are you watching the warriors practice? Are you looking for your future husband?"

The shock and panic she felt when she first heard his voice changed to anger with his mocking tone. Fists clenched and her eyes met his. "I want to be a warrior," she replied, a six-year-old girl to a soldier of twenty years or more.

"But why," he asked, "do you want to be a warrior?" His gentle humor at her words grated on her pride.

"To kill the enemies of Eltrand. To serve the god Yrdon. To carry on the noble line of Ishdinar." Her rote answer clearly took him by surprise, because he had no response at first. Then his smile reappeared.

"I will make you a deal," he promised. "Once you pass the age of consent, I will train you at my own castle until you reach the first level of combat. If you want to continue after that, I will leave it in the gods' hands."

The words were so unexpected that she couldn't understand their meaning at first. Then Shazia grinned and clapped her hands together in delight. His responding smile, she was to learn later, was something of which to be wary.

♦♦♦

Rabanar's face held many more lines than it had sixteen years before when he had offered to train Shazia to be a warrior. His hair had more grey than seven years before, when Ibin had gotten her drunk and a gypsy had told her a fortune. But it was still the same face, and his smile had not faded. "The Falloyda will see you now," he murmured.

She didn't know whether to take the smile as a good sign or bad. The smile was his trademark. He smiled at all times, including when he killed.

Shazia bowed her head lower. Surprisingly, her peripheral vision saw his palms join and he bowed his head in return. Her breath caught in her chest at his gesture of respect, and her head shot up and turned automatically to watch his slow, measuring steps as he walked away. It was only when his path turned to the right and she lost him to sight that she drew a great deal of air into her lungs and faced the council chambers alone.

Her heart was racing. Rabanar had honored her with his gesture. It was the salute of a lower officer to one of higher rank. What did it mean? Did it mean what she hoped?

She cleared her mind of all thoughts, as if she was going into battle. She would find out soon enough.

It was the first time she had ever been in Lisardon, the capital city of Eltrand. The first time she had ever visited the palace. The first time she would see the Falloyda, the princes of the blood. There had not been a king, a true king, in over a century. A monarch, like the nobility, only earned his title in battle. While the royal blood passed from son to son, until a royal was victorious in war, he could not join the line of kings.

Her eyes adjusted to the darkness of the room once she passed from the window-filled hall to the near-blackness of the torch-lit council chamber. Her eyes rolled from side to side to judge the feel of the men and women in the room.

She was the only female in uniform. Lining the walls, like glittering shadows of the men seated in a row in front of them, were the women of court. Their clothing would not survive a single horseback ride, and the jewels and coifs of their hair would be blown askew with the slightest breath of wind.

The women stood behind their husbands and lords. But whereas the men refrained from excessive motion or speech, their wives were a sea of movement, every breath they took eliciting a thousand glimmers from their fancy costumes, every flick of fan or glove creating a whirlwind of lace and velvet. The low murmuring of their voices were like wind chimes in a lazy summer breeze.

At the end of the hall stood an empty seat on a raised dais. No one could sit on the dais or on that throne except the king.

With the back legs of their chairs touching the edge of the platform, three men sat waiting for her. She stopped several body-lengths in front of them. The middle man spoke.

"Welcome to the fair capital of Eltrand, Shazia de Laiyer. If you were any other warrior, there would be no question in the minds of the court and council gathered here today. You have been in the arena and have bested all challengers. Quite a few challengers, I might add." The quiet humor in the man's voice almost gave her hope.

"But you are not any other warrior," he continued gravely. "And in all the chronicles of Eltrand, there is no other case such as this one, of a woman joining the highest ranks of the army. If you are thinking of Lissar," and she had been thinking of Lissar, the goddess-queen, who was a shining example of precedence, "you cannot assume that we will take her actions as a case for yours. You are not Lissar. She was an exception, a warrior with divine guidance. Since the gods have not spoken, we judge you have no such divinity to aid you."

She realized her head was sinking lower with each word, as if the cadence of his voice were blows, and consciously halted its decline. A warrior obeyed orders and the commands of her superiors, she reminded herself. Slowly, she raised her head again.

"But . . ." The man paused. His thin lips turned down at the corners and his teeth bared in an expression that did not resemble a smile. "But more than one noble of the court has spoken on your behalf. And it would be foolish of me to ignore that times are changing more rapidly than ever before.

"You are not the gods-blessed Lissar," he repeated. "But you may be a symbol of her reign. Eltrand has far to go to recapture its golden age. If we do not attempt to regain it now, we may never get a second chance." Shazia saw that the two men flanking the speaker were staring at her with nearly identical smiles. Their expressions were not pleasant. "And so I declare before the council that you have won the title of First Rank of the Armies of Eltrand."

She felt as if her heart had exploded. The breath she had been holding was released in a quiet hiss that only the three men could hear.

The Falloyda's next words rang out in the densely-packed hall: "Come forward, Shazia de Laiyer."

Her feet moved forward without needing her brain's advice. In the Falloyda's hand was a silver pendant made in the shape of a star, a small copy of Yrdun's most holy relic. As she bent so he could place it around her neck, he spoke so only the two men near him and she could hear his words.

"If it was my decision alone, you would have been whipped and sent back to the kitchens long before now." He was in the process of putting the chain around her neck, and his hands were on either side of her throat.

She stiffened, prepared to fend off any attack he might make. Shazia didn't care who he was. But his hands loosened and he pulled them back to his sides. He was still smiling, an expression he held for the court to see.

She stepped back, bowed once more to acknowledge the public honor he had given her. But she was sure he saw the anger in her eyes, for he paled slightly. She could tell, even seated as he was, that he was not a large man. She would tower over him if he were standing. But he gathered himself together to complete the ritual.

"Go from this hall with Yrdun's blessing."

♦♦♦

Ibin was waiting for her outside the main doors. How he had managed it, she had no idea. As far as she knew, he was supposed to be back at Castle Var during his father's absence from there.

He threw his arms around her and thumped her heartily on the back. It didn't seem to bother him that he had to reach up to do so, as he had ever since her eighteenth birthday.

"Let me look at you," he said, pulling back. He eyed the star on her breast, identical to the one he wore around his throat. "Looks better on you than me," he said, flicking his pendant disrespectfully with one finger.

"Stop," she said, laughing. "This is serious, you know."

He grinned. "Of course I know. Want to get a drink?"

Her constitution had improved since her fifteenth birthday, but drinking had never topped her list of favorite activities. "Want to spar a few rounds?" she asked, anticipating his groan.

He didn't disappoint her. "That's all you think about, Shaz," he said. "Time to live a little."

"You live too much," she retorted.

"Okay, let's split the difference," he said, slinging an arm around her shoulders, which made him stand on the balls of his feet, and caused her to hunch down to accommodate him. "There's a traveling band of entertainers . . ."

"Yrdun forbid," she said. "Tell you what—you go out, have a great time in the city, and tell me all about it tomorrow. I'll go back to your family's townhouse and get some sleep before I have to come back here tomorrow morning to get my assignment."

"Spoilsport." But he was grinning as he said it. "All right. I suppose we could do that. Here, let me walk you back."

She eyed him up and down skeptically. "I don't need your protection," she muttered. "I can take care of myself."

"It's not for you!" he exclaimed, dropping his arm and placing a fluttering hand upon his chest. "It's for me. No one would dare accost me if I'm at your side. I feel safer already, knowing you're here."

He had her laughing until she had to hold her sides. "Oh, Ibin, I'm going to miss you. I wish we could be posted together."

He mock-shuddered. "Yrdun forfend," he said. "The day I face border duty is the day you can put an arrow through my eye."

"Deal," she grinned.

♦♦♦

The next morning, Rabanar stood at her side outside the council chambers. He said nothing, but it was not his job to make small talk.

When the doors finally opened, she barely noticed the rustling court ladies, the foppish men. She marched straight forward to the three Falloyda and bowed. Rabanar bowed beside her.

When she straightened, though, a spear of doubt twisted into her stomach. While the Falloyda had not been pleasant yesterday and danger had ridden their actions, today they seemed positively gleeful.

"We have sad tidings," the middle man said. "There has been an attack."

Shazia resisted the urge to glance over at Rabanar. She felt, rather than saw, Rabanar stiffen at her side.

"What sort of attack?" he asked.

The Falloyda shook his head, but his lips were turned up at the corners. "A personal attack on one of Yrdun's most faithful followers. I am sorry to inform you, sir, but your son has been killed."

Shazia wondered if Rabanar was wearing his signature grin. It was a mask, she knew. But sometimes masks were helpful. The spear of doubt was twisting inside of her, and she knew that her face had frozen. She couldn't seem to move, not even open her mouth to speak.

"That is sad news," Rabanar said. If he was feeling anything, it did not show in his voice. "Which son of mine?"

"The middle one. What was his name?" The Falloyda turned to his brother seated to the right. The other prince murmured something. "Oh, yes," the middle Falloyda continued in his loud, mocking voice. "Ibin de Rabanar."

♦ ♦ ♦

Time must have passed. Words must have been exchanged. But the next Shazia knew, she was outside the palace doors with Rabanar by her side.

"They will pay for this," he said coldly.

"They, sir?" Her voice sounded listless to her own ears.

His look was speculative when he turned her. But she did not ask her question again.

Abruptly, he nodded and strode off, leaving her standing by herself on the front steps of the palace.

Aside from the guards, a steady stream of people moved in and out of the wide-open doors. Shazia moved to the side of the traffic flow and leaned against a sharply-ridged pillar. She put her head back and stared up into the clear blue sky.

Ibin is dead.

No, he can't be.

They wouldn't have said it if it isn't true.

How can he be dead? He's my closest friend.

He can't be dead.

But they said he is.

If only I had been there to protect him, he wouldn't be dead . . .

Her thoughts circled, snarling at one another like rabid dogs. She realized abruptly that she hadn't even heard her posting assignment—she had no idea where she was supposed to go, who she was supposed to see. After hearing that Ibin was gone, there was a blank space, a void.

A day ago, she had stood on these steps and laughed so hard with Ibin that her sides had hurt.

She blinked and turned away. Her feet felt like bricks, but she moved them.

Ibin is dead.

She found herself nodding her head, the echo of Rabanar's words overtaking her thoughts.

They will pay for this.

♦♦♦

When she opened the door to Rabanar's townhouse, she didn't know what to expect. Certainly not what she found.

The foyer had been cleared of all furniture except for a table draped in a white cloth. On top of the table was a body.

She covered her face with one palm, turned away. It wasn't until a hand gripped her shoulder that she realized the foyer wasn't empty, hadn't been empty. Instead, it was filled with soldiers.

The hand on her shoulder belonged to Rabanar. "You have a choice," he told her. Her eyes moved beyond him and focused on the faces in the room. "With us or against us."

Past Rabanar's shoulder were ranks upon ranks of officers. Some battle-scarred, some little older than her. Over there was the last First Rank from five years ago, Almarre de Salza. Closer by was Harpett, who was old even when she was young, but now seemed to have reached an indeterminate middle age. There were many more whose faces she didn't recognize or whose names escaped her.

Rabanar must have been planning this for some time. This was not a direct response to his son's death. Ibin was the excuse, not the catalyst.

"Why?" she asked instead.

Rabanar shook his head. "It has been decades since a king has sat on the throne," he said. "And over a century since Lissar, the goddess-queen, led Eltrand to its golden age. It is time for us to return to what we once were."

A new calm descended upon her. "Is that why you agreed to train me?" she asked. "To seize power from the Falloyda?" She nodded her head at Ibin's body, but tried not to look. That unmoving face seemed like sacrilege, more so than anything else she had ever seen or heard. That someone so alive, so vital, should have died so young. "What happened to him? And don't try to tell me it was the Falloyda. Even they wouldn't be so bold."

Rabanar was grinning, but it was an expression that did nothing to reassure her. "The Falloyda are powerless, but Ibin couldn't see that. He was very vocal in his support of them." Rabanar rested a heavy hand on her shoulder, and she shuddered under his touch and the look in his eyes. "As a symbol, you bring hope. Why do you think so many have joined us? You are a sign of change."

"If the Falloyda didn't kill Ibin—" Her words died in her mouth. Past Rabanar's shoulder, she saw the one person she never thought to see again. "Father," she breathed.

Laiyer nodded his head at her, but didn't speak. When she had left home, he had vowed never to speak to her again.

He still had no words to give her. Even if they were on the same side, even if they fought back to back, he would not break that vow sworn before the gods. She could see that now, that same stubbornness that she carried within her, that had pushed her to become what she had become.

Seeing that, her purpose crystalized. Her mind flashed back, stretched past the death of her closest friend, and settled on a moment when she sat in a tent and a gypsy had fumbled a card of fortune.

"I will stand with you," she said clearly. Loudly, so that it carried throughout the room.

And so they told her their plans, and they buried Rabanar's son the next morning. But it would take one more week before they would be able to lead the insurrection, since they waited for their allies to journey from the far reaches of Eltrand to join them in overthrowing the Falloyda.

Right after the funeral, she told Rabanar, "I need some time to clear my head." He nodded, clapped her once more on the shoulder, and let her go.

Shazia had never been to so large a city. Her world had been smaller, had been contained to the manor house where she had been born, and Rabanar's estate. But with Ibin at her side, her world had never felt small.

He had been a traveler, though. He would go on long treks throughout the countryside, sent on various errands by his father. But always he would return, and he would share with her tales of his journeys and the people he had met and the things he had done. Always, he came back.

The Falloyda didn't expect her return. When she strode into the council chambers, there was a rustle of sound that followed the rumble of her boots across the floor.

"What is the meaning of this?" The Falloyda who had given her the star pendant scraped his chair on the floor as he cowered before her.

Again, she saw the cards laid out in front of her from half a dozen years before. Soldier, traveler, and death. Or, just maybe, she would find a different path to walk.

"Change is coming," she replied, her voice the odd echo of a traitor. A soldier's death, she understood. Murder—the murder of his son, no less—she never would. Rabanar had lost her forever.

"Change is coming," she repeated. "There are those disloyal to the crown who seek to overthrow you. And you can either be a force of change—with *me*—or against it."

She took a deep breath. Here was where her path diverged.

"I have made my choice," she said, without regret. "Now, the choice is yours."

♦ ♦ ♦ PENNED ♦ ♦ ♦

Author's Note: *This is perhaps my oldest publication in existence aside from stories published by my college journal—this story originally saw the light of day in 2004. I wrote it shortly after the Jayson Blair scandal broke in 2003, where a lot of the discussion about his plagiarized articles for the* New York Times *evolved into discussions about race.*

Fifteen years later, racism is still very much alive and kicking in today's America, and so while this story might be a bit dated, I wanted to re-examine the themes it brought up and see if the message still holds resonance for today's readers. This was originally a commentary about how the easiest solutions may not always have the intended consequences, even with the best of intentions. Perhaps the message is still relevant; perhaps not. I'll let you be the judge of that.

AN OLDER CROWD GATHERED AT the bar during the middle of the week. As Michael started up the outside stairs to his place over the pub, he heard the word at the edge of his senses.

No white man should be saying that word to him. To his face or to his back.

He half-turned his head. There were three or four men standing in the bar's small parking lot, one smoking a fat stogie. The pungent smell filled his nose. He recognized Gary, the husband of the newspaper's editor—the newspaper where Michael worked. Gary's eyes met his, but flickered as he sucked in a mouthful of smoke. The other men took their cue and turned away.

The word was not repeated. But Michael knew one of them had said it. They knew he had heard it. He climbed he last three steps, unlocked his door, and went inside.

The studio apartment was dark, but there wasn't a need for a light. He slumped against the locked door as the tension drained from his muscles, and had dark thoughts about the small southern town's white residents.

♦♦♦

The thin letter began with the familiar phrase: "Thank you for your resume, but . . ." Michael turned over the envelope and fingered the postmark date. Barely a week before, he'd sent his resume to the *New York Times*. "Hardly enough time to open my application," he said to the orange and white tabby on his lap, followed by a long stroke from the tip of her ears to the base of her tail. "Or to read past the name of my state school."

He carefully folded the letter and put it back in the envelope. Gently, so as not to disturb the cat, he reached under the table and groped for the thick binder. He tucked the latest letter on top of the pile and casually tossed the binder back under the table.

He opened up the *NY Times* over his morning coffee and scanned the headlines. "War, war, terrorism, war," he murmured. "Now, here's something different." The tabby preened under the sound of his voice.

"Self-Actualization. Realize your dreams by changing your state of mind. Begin with this exercise: every day, write an affirmative sentence about yourself twenty times. It can be about something you want to accomplish, or something that you really like about yourself. If you don't begin to feel better and accomplish more in your life after two weeks, then no harm done. But if you do begin to see a difference in your life—

"Then what?" Michael snorted. "Buy his book?" The cat, objecting to the harsh tone, jumped from his lap and flounced over to the unmade futon bed. Michael folded the paper, gulped his coffee, and grabbed his jacket from the chair. He would be late to the newspaper office if he didn't hurry. As he strode down the sidewalk, he thought hopefully that if he ever was hired as a journalist for the *Times*, he would write serious articles, not trash like that.

♦♦♦

It wouldn't work, Michael assured himself a couple of days later as he sat alone at his kitchen table with a blank sheet of paper and a pen. It was just some hippie trying to make money off his fellow baby boomers.

On the other hand, it didn't hurt to try, he reasoned. Even if it was a scam, at least he wasn't paying five dollars an hour for Miss Cleo to tell him he'd marry a supermodel.

Thinking about his job, his walk home after work, and the word that had followed him to his apartment door, he decided that he wanted to be able to make a difference. He wrote: "There is power in my pen."

He scanned the sentence. Even if this came true, he wouldn't know because it was too ambiguous. He wrote a second sentence: "I will be hired by the *New York Times*."

Whoops, he had changed verb tense in the second sentence. He crossed out "will be" and wrote "am."

"Hired by the *Times* to do what?" he thought. He didn't want to be a janitor. He crossed out "hired by" and wrote "a journalist for."

He reread what he had written: "There is power in my pen. I am a journalist for the *New York Times*." He wrote the two sentences nineteen more times. Putting down the pen, he stared at the crabbed, black lines scrawled across the sheet.

"I must be crazy!" he muttered. But he left the paper and pen sitting on his kitchen table and went to bed.

♦♦♦

The alarm went off and he groaned. It felt like he had barely shut his eyes. He hit the beeping clock by reflex, then looked at the time. "Christ!" he growled. "Who the hell set my alarm?"

He stumbled to his feet and noticed by the shallow light of the bedside lamp that something was different. Where was the bathroom door? When he flicked on the overhead light, he leaned against the doorjamb as his groggy mind tried to assimilate the information his eyes were sending it. “What the—”

His furniture was no longer mismatched hand-me-downs. The king-sized bed from which he’d woken had a mahogany headboard with a matching nightstand. A flat-panel television faced the bed. Next to a closet with suits hanging side by side was a half-open doorway that revealed a gleaming bathtub set against a spotless black floor.

He took in a deep breath. “Holy shit, I must be dreaming,” he said out loud. What do people do in a dream? The pinch themselves to see if they’re awake.

He was awake. He pinched harder. Oh, yeah, definitely awake.

Running to the windows, he yanked up the grey blinds and looked out. “Shit, holy shit!” he repeated to his reflection. The city that never sleeps, his dream city: New York. He was in an apartment in the city.

He sat down on the bed and took a deep breath. How had this happened? He needed coffee to think. He stood and left the bedroom, turning on the lights as he crossed the living room. On the far side of the room was a half-counter bar opening into a kitchen. The lights of the city glimmered through the windows of a small breakfast nook. On the table was a piece of paper and a pen.

His fingers flicked the light switch as if this place were home. The piece of paper flared white in the sudden illumination. He laughed briefly as his legs shook underneath him, and he managed to pull out a chair before sitting down.

The paper was blank.

♦♦♦

He found that if he let his mind wander, he had dim memories of another life, like remembering a drunken party the morning after. His New York life was like something he had heard happen to someone else, but every agonizing detail of the life he had lived as a small town journalist was clear.

As he tried to wrap his mind around what had happened, he found himself dressed in a suit at the door of his apartment. Patting his pockets, he found he had picked up keys and a wallet. He let his mind blank out and found himself walking down the street, his arm raised, hailing a cab.

He didn't have much to say at the early morning meeting, but no one seemed to notice. After the conference, he found his desk and sat drinking coffee and staring at his laptop screen.

The cell rang in his pocket and jolted him out of his reflection. Putting down his coffee, he pulled out his phone and looked at it, but didn't take the call. After it rang five times, it became quiet and he pocketed it again.

What could he say if confronted with someone who wanted something from the him who lived in this reality? His memories were still a blur. His life had changed because of what he had written on that paper last night. Now he had to track down why.

It began with the article. He needed to find out who was responsible for the article.

The screensaver on his laptop had a scrolling message: "If you're reading this, you're not working hard enough." His home page was, of course, the *Times*. His username and password pulled up an access screen that brought him to the

Times archives. He set the search parameters for roughly three weeks with the keywords: self-actualization. The first hit under the entertainment section was the correct article, but the name on the article couldn't be right. He opened the web page to be sure. No way.

The details of his New York "memories" seemed to be taking focus and the small town of Greensville was beginning to get fuzzy. He looked at his watch. He had woken up five and a half hours before.

He remembered now the work he had put into the self-actualization article. As far as he remembered, it had been straight-forward interviews and research. He mentally cursed his fading memories of his other life, because he couldn't remember the name of the original author of the article.

Would it matter, in this other life? he wondered. *He* had written the article.

He didn't realize how much time he'd killed until there was a soft laugh behind him. He swiveled his chair to see his editor's grinning face.

"Seeking inspiration?" Angie asked. "Because I've been watching you for about five minutes, and you've done nothing but twirl that pen and stare at your screensaver. Aren't you supposed to be working?"

He grinned. "I *am* working. My next article is the shocking expose about computer screensavers. Big Brother's putting subliminal messages in them."

"Oh?" Raised eyebrow. "And what's the government trying to sell us?"

"A tax-cut for big business, with a side of fries. Speaking of which, is it time for lunch already?" He grabbed his jacket and slung it on as they headed for the elevator, chatting.

♦♦♦

He threw his keys and wallet onto the table by the door of his apartment. The self-actualization article had been a dead end. Where did that leave him?

He grabbed a beer from the fridge while staring at the blank piece of paper and pen on the kitchen table. He had written the night before: "There is power in my pen. I am a journalist for the New York Times."

It had come true, but not as he had intended, as something to happen in the future. The present tense of the sentence had come true. But in order for this present reality to happen, it had changed his past.

He shook his head. It was too complicated. What if he wrote something for an article and his opinion changed the world around him again? He needed to find out the rules. He could end up being unable to write ever again for fear of what would happen.

Grabbing a chair, he sat down before the white paper and picked up the pen. But what should he write?

It should be something easy to verify instantly. He looked around him and smiled as he realized what had been missing since he woke up that morning.

"I own an orange and white cat." Twenty sentences later, he capped the pen and set it beside the piece of paper.

♦♦♦

"Mrrr? Merrrow?" A rough tongue across his chin reinforced the beeping alarm. His flailing hand found the light switch and his eyes cracked open to see a familiar face peering down at him. His laughter scared the cat. With an offended flounce of her tail, she stalked off the large mahogany bed and headed in the direction of the kitchen to await breakfast.

♦♦♦

He had a strange shiver of déjà vu when he sat down at the conference table at the crack-of-dawn meeting one Friday a couple of weeks later. It was the same type of meeting that had begun his new, actualized life at his dream job in New York. Sipping coffee and listening with half an ear to the usual story ideas being shot down left and right by the editor, he was daydreaming about last Friday night when he had met a girl who had taught him what all night long really meant when—

"If our Mr. Garvey cares to join the conversation, we might be able to get some work done today." He sat up abruptly at Angie's reprimand, nearly spilling his lukewarm drink.

He smiled, trying for composure. "Sorry, just thinking about the quotes from the Philman article. I'm here."

"Yesterday's school shootings," she replied without missing a beat. "And we aren't looking for melodrama. Let's have some stats and facts. We're hurting for staff PR, so even if it takes all your waking hours, it'd better be good."

Michael looked around the table at all the eyes staring at him. So he had been daydreaming a little this morning and gotten caught. It wasn't a crime. Nor was he the only African-American reporter who worked at the *Times*. He hadn't even known the guy who had been making up the facts for his stories—the guy who had been caught and fired several weeks before Michael's self-actualized life had even started.

"I already have a lot on my plate, Angie," he replied stiffly. "Are you sure that this piece is right for me?" The story was like nothing he had done previously for the entertainment section of the paper. The only connection that he could see was that the shootings had occurred in a predominantly black neighborhood and he normally wrote about African-American culture.

"Gang bangers not your cup of tea?" she asked sarcastically. He clenched his jaw against an angry retort. Everybody had been on edge since the shit hit the fan a few weeks back. He tried to calm down and affect the same lazy drawl as before.

"Sure, I'll take it. I just expect a comfy four-poster installed next to my desk, since I'll be working twenty-four seven to meet deadline."

This brought a smile or laugh from everyone at the table. "Yes, poor overworked Michael," snorted Angie in a lighter tone. "Pulling all the weight while the rest of us sit on our butts and relax." Michael pulled his lips up into a grin to match the room's lightening change of attitude from hostile to jovial. But as he looked at the light-skinned faces around the room, he seethed.

♦♦♦

After getting home very late that night, he sat on his black leather couch and stroked his cat from nose to tail, trying to relax enough to sleep. The animal's warmth and purring were comforting, but Michael's neck and back ached with tension.

He stood up abruptly and the tabby squawked as she was catapulted to the floor. Michael marched to the kitchen where the paper and pen waited.

Seated at the table, his mind was filled with a thousand different things to write. Co-workers had begun avoiding him since the other journalist was fired, as if black skin and shoddy work walked hand in hand. Today was the last straw.

The problem was not where to start, but where to end. He was tired of racism, but he wasn't the only person on the planet who had felt such hatred directed at him. He was one of many people who lived with the aftermath of years of slavery and oppression. If he helped one person of color specifically by name, it left hundreds out. No, millions or even billions. His mind raced to AIDS in South Africa, war in the Middle East, conflicts in Asia.

He found his teeth locked around the pen and eased back to tap the table thoughtfully with one finger. He needed to solve one problem at a time. Where did it all begin?

He thought back to that one night as a small-town journalist in another life, and the man calling out a name to his back, a name steeped in racial hatred dating back to the days of slavery.

Michael straightened in his chair, an idea beginning to form. No, he couldn't. It was too radical. He couldn't do it.

His heart raced. The pen touched the paper. He wrote the sentence down once, a second time, then another. His pen scribbled ferociously to write it down again and again and again, before he could take it back. He was afraid to reread it, but forced himself to say it aloud.

"Slavery does not exist."

The pain was gone. He felt light and free. The pen hit the table as he stood abruptly and laughed. He jumped around his apartment until he was out of breath and had to collapse on his couch, panting and grinning.

It was Friday night. Because he had been so depressed, he had canceled a date. Now he called up his friends and invited them to a night on the town.

"I'm celebrating something," he told them mysteriously. "I'll tell you everything tomorrow."

♦♦♦

His head was pounding. He tried to move and felt as if his body belonged to someone else, someone who was beaten up and left for dead. His head felt worse. God Almighty, he felt like crap.

What was that smell? Had he been sick? He groaned and the sound of his own voice made his stomach churn. His eyes opened as he pushed his pained body up, to get to the bathroom. He made it through the door right before brown liquid gushed from his throat onto the dirt.

Dirt? His head was foggy, but it shouldn't be *that* foggy.

The bright sun was killing him, but he managed to squint at his surroundings. Trees lined the clearing in which mud and palm-thatched houses stood in a semi-circle. By the sun, it was about noon. In the shade of the palms, there were a few women wearing red wrap-around dresses sorting through the contents of two baskets.

"Holy shit," he murmured.

His hand flew to his mouth because the words hadn't been English. He was glad he watched Discovery Channel, because he suddenly knew where he was.

Panic made the pain in his stomach and head remarkably easy to ignore. He rushed back inside the hut and looked for the two objects. They were next to his bedding.

He grabbed the pen and paper and went outside again, where the bright light made the paper a glaring white. Uncapping the pen, he placed the point against the paper.

"Slavery exists," he said out loud in the language that sounded foreign to his ears.

Nothing happened with the pen on paper. "Slavery exists," he repeated.

Still nothing. He glared at the paper. "Goddamn it, slavery exists!" he shouted. The pen didn't move.

He couldn't make it move, because he didn't know how to write.

The past life was already distant and fading fast. All that was left was an Africa that had never known slavery, an Africa that had never helped Europe bring slaves to the New World to create an empire.

He dropped the pen. The paper followed—bright, white, and completely useless.

♦ ♦ ♦ THE LOST CHILDREN ♦ ♦ ♦

WHEN THE MIDWIVES CAME RUNNING out the door, crying, Minos rushed into the birthing room. His wife already had the two babies at her breast. The one on the left waved her hands gently as she nursed, but did not turn her head to look up at him. Her long-lashed eyes were closed against the brown hair covering her face, her bovine lips suckling intently. The one on the right kicked his hooves, blinking his sleepy human eyes at the king standing frozen in the doorway. Minos stared at Pasiphaë with horror.

"They are born from your arrogance," his wife told him wearily. There was a note of triumph in her voice. "You would not honor Poseidon by sacrificing the white bull. And I have fallen in love with the bull as deeply as you have."

Minos looked at the two half-creatures, part human and part calf. "More deeply, it would seem," he said. Dazed, he slowly started to walk towards her. "I will kill these monsters. And you," he added belatedly. "For making a fool of me and sinning with the god's beast."

"The bull was Poseidon's gift to you, but you would not sacrifice him as the god commanded. If you had killed him when you were supposed to, this would never have happened. The goddess Aphrodite has already come to bless these children. Would you argue with the gods?"

"I have before," said Minos. He was human, and he had made mistakes. He should have done what the gods had told him, but he had, as his wife said, been arrogant. He shrank back against the wall, feeling suddenly old and spent of his fury. "Very well. But expect nothing more from me except for your lives."

Pasiphaë raised her chin. "I have never expected more. And you have given to me the nothing you promised, over and over again."

♦♦♦

By the king's decree, the children were allowed to live, and indeed, their lives were peaceful. They stayed in Pasiphaë's rooms at first. The girl, Agaphya, was a gentle and docile daughter. She did exactly what she was told, but couldn't manipulate her large cow's tongue to speak human language, and so remained mute. Her brother, Asterion, grew at an alarming rate, the same as any bull. Within half a year, it was hard for him to enter through the narrow doorway leading to his mother's room. Within a year, he was forced to spend his days outside, in a covered tent rigged up for him in the courtyard with the assistance of his mother's handmaids.

Although his body grew at a bull's rate, his head grew at a human's rate, so he had the small baby face of a one-year-old perched atop his strong bull's neck.

Agaphya refused to be separated from her brother. If she was taken away for even so much as a moment, she would wobble her large cow's head atop her small baby's neck and low and low endlessly. The sound was inescapable, her moaning cow cries impossible to hush. Finally, their mother allowed the girl to toddle out to her brother and sleep against his warm side at night. The girl spent her days riding on Asterion as he walked around the courtyard, her legs split wide over the expanse of his broad back. He was careful of his hooves around the tiny girl when she walked on her own feet, and one could tell where his sister was standing simply by the direction in which he pointed his face at any given time. They were like one creature separated into two bodies—or, more correctly, two creatures meant to be one.

The king's subjects grew so used to having these two as a fixture at the palace that it sometimes came as a shock when visiting dignitaries expressed fear or disgust at seeing them for the first time. The only one who never seemed to accept them was Minos, who took pains to avoid the main courtyard. When he was forced to cross it, he would hurry by and never look up at the two children-beasts there. And they would watch him silently, never speaking or drawing attention to themselves. Their mother had told them about Minos. What she had said was best left unrepeated.

Twelve years passed, and Asterion's face lengthened, grew larger and more proportionate with his bull's body. Agaphya's huge cow head no longer tended to overtip her if she walked too quickly, for she grew taller and broader. By age sixteen, the two halves of their nature seemed to settle into a complementary whole, a blending together of things as intended by the gods.

But the more content the two siblings seemed, the more the king's face grew wrathful every time he happened to spot them. When he overheard his counselors speaking about these two creatures as "The Minotaurs," some sort of benevolent symbol for the city, he was furious. This was *his* city, not a place for the foul offspring of his wife's adultery. He needed to do something, and that something came about through listening to his wife, incidentally enough.

He hadn't touched Pasiphaë since the birth. Not brushed a sleeve past hers or put a hand on her skin. He had barely seen her. But at important state functions, he needed a queen as hostess for the appearance of things, and so several times a year, he would summon her to attend court. She always came and fulfilled her duties impeccably. But the slow burn of hatred in his heart engendered by her deceitful presence took weeks to disperse again.

This time was no exception. Even though he had summoned her, upon seeing Pasiphaë's still-beautiful face, Minos was overwhelmed for a moment with rage. He had to take several deep breaths before he could speak. "We have visitors from the mainland," he told her.

"Very well."

"I will send you the details via your handmaiden. Tomorrow is the feast. I want you to show them all honors."

"Of course. Is there anything else?"

The presumption of the woman! He seethed, but finally shook his head. He did not trust his voice. She turned and left without saying anything else, without once meeting his eyes.

The next night, with the envoys of kings at his side, he couldn't help but hear the words of his wife as she conversed with one of the ambassadors two seats away. "I would never dare!" she laughed—flirtatiously, he thought.

"It is not as scary as it is made out to be," grinned the man. He toyed with the grapes on his plate, as if giving his hands something to do while his attention was diverted by a beautiful woman. "In fact, it was over quite quickly."

"I have always wondered about the oracle." Pasiphaë's voice lowered, and Minos couldn't hear what was said next.

"Yes, I know. I saw them as I came in," replied the ambassador.

That very night, Minos commanded his ships be readied for sailing in the morning. If that man could find answers at Delphi's oracle, so could he. He was a king, after all. And the gods bent special favor upon his kind.

♦♦♦

When he returned, Minos brought shiploads of new people with him, crowds of architects and slaves. They set to work immediately. The oracle had told him to build a maze underneath his palace, a massive cage for the two unnatural godspawn creatures. Once that was done, he was to leave them trapped in the center.

Work proceeded quickly. He was unsurprised to see Pasiphaë when she eventually came to visit him, her face as pale as cheese.

"You can't mean to do this. They are *children*."

"They are monsters," he told her coldly. "I should have done this long before."

She pleaded, she begged for their lives. He relented enough that a small chute was built in the center of the palace, so food and drink could be dropped down for those below. "This is your responsibility," he told her. "I will have no one help you in this task. You must prepare the food with your own hands and bring it to them. If you fail in that, I will have rocks thrown down instead, and the entrance sealed."

The queen bowed her head. "Thank you for your generosity, King Midos." She could not quite contain the bitterness in her tone.

"Be careful, wife," he told her. "Lest I force their adulterous mother to join them. Then there would be no one left to feed you."

Pasiphaë bowed her head lower. This time, she did not trust her voice to speak. At her apparent humility, he let her take leave of his presence.

♦♦♦

When her children were blindfolded, twenty strong men had to restrain Asterion as he used every bit of his bull's strength to try and escape. Agaphya, docile as always, meekly allowed her head to be covered with a sack and followed the hands that guided her. Pasiphaë wept as her children were led into the labyrinth, but made no move to stop the soldiers who took them. She knew King Midos's eyes were on her. She knew, but did not care, except to fervently remind herself that her children would die without her. She needed to stay strong of heart.

Each day before the sun rose, Pasiphaë trekked down to the marketplace and purchased the freshest foodstuffs she could find. Then back to the palace kitchens, where she would spend hours chopping and stirring, creating simple but nutritious fare. She would tie the meals up in a cloth and lower them on a string through the palace chute. When she felt the tug on the other end, she counted a double handful of numbers, and then brought the string back up, with only the cloth at the end of it, now emptied of viands.

After a year passed, King Midos summoned her again. "There is a delegation from Athens," he told her. "They have spoken to the oracle."

"What now?" she asked warily.

"Plague," he replied. "The oracle told them to sacrifice a boy and girl to the creatures underneath our city."

"Sacrifice? Creatures? They are no more violent than I am! They are children, still, and you have imprisoned them. What have they ever done to you?"

Midos loomed over her. "They were born," he said. "That is enough." There was nothing she could argue against that. He continued, "You must lead the sacrifices to the center of the maze."

"How am I to do that? I have never been inside the labyrinth. I don't know my way to the center."

For the first time, Midos smiled. It was not a friendly expression. "You will learn."

♦♦♦

In the end, her handmaiden came up with the answer. "String," the woman said. "Tie a piece to the entrance to guide you back through any wrong turnings."

It worked like a charm. Although the boy and girl from Athens were frightened after many hours traveling through the labyrinth, and upon finally seeing the two creatures who awaited them, Pasiphaë managed to reassure them. "These two will not hurt you," she told the sacrifices. "They are my children."

The Athenian delegation, satisfied when she came back by herself, went on their way. Pasiphaë sent even more food down the chutes to care for the extra mouths. A year later, the Athenians returned.

"Plague? The oracle?" she guessed when Midos summoned her.

"Yes," he said without preamble. She led the two new children to the center of the maze and spent many hours of each day after that preparing food for the prisoners in the labyrinth. A year later, the ships returned.

This time, Midos declared that he would celebrate their arrival with a feast. The oracle had told the Athenians that this third time would permanently end the plague that had troubled them. Pasiphaë sat next to the ambassador, the young son of the Athenian king, and spoke with him throughout the long night. Afterwards, she took to her bed, exhausted from the celebrations. Tomorrow, she would lead the last of the children into the maze.

But the next morning, she was feverish and crying out at the pain. Midos, arriving to summon her to the maze, looked down at his wife and saw the telltale boils rising to the surface of her skin. Pasiphaë was insensible, unaware that he was even standing over her. "Tend to her," he told her handmaiden. "And send the ambassador to me."

The young man came immediately. Theseus, Midos recalled. "The queen has fallen to Athen's plague," he said. The young man appeared startled.

"But the oracle said…"

"Only one thing can cure her. An end to this dreadful disease. Bring the final sacrifices to the center of the maze. Do not come back until you have done so."

"But I do not know the way. Only the queen knows."

"Do not trouble me with useless details. Ask her, if you are so inclined."

With a sinking feeling, the prince knocked at the entrance to her rooms. The handmaiden allowed him into the queen's chambers, but Pasiphaë was tossing back and forth and couldn't answer his questions.

"I know a way," said a soft voice behind him. He turned to see the queen's handmaiden, a woman a little older than Pasiphaë. "String," she explained to him.

As he went into the labyrinth, Theseus took the children with one hand and held the string with the other. Although he made many wrong turnings through the twisting corridors of the stone maze, hours later, he made the final turning and saw a sea of light.

Or so it seemed, after such a long time in the darkness. At the center of the enormous cavern at the labyrinth's end, a small fire was burning. Four children sat around its perimeter, black with smoke and filth. They cowered back at his sudden appearance, at the rage on his face when he saw them. Here were all the sacrifices demanded by the oracle. No wonder Athens had continued to suffer plague, if all these sacrifices still lived. It was the deepest betrayal of the gods.

Suddenly, he heard a sound to his left and looked over to see two monstrous creatures approaching him. One thundered towards him like a galloping horse, and he dropped the string he was holding and reached for his sword.

When he emerged from the entrance to the labyrinth hours later, having followed the string back to its source, the soldiers at the entrance gaped at him. Theseus wiped a bloody hand across his face, but it didn't improve his appearance. One of the men at the entrance tentatively asked, "Were you successful?"

Theseus looked down at his bloody hands. "Yes," he said shortly. "They are all dead."

The man's eyes widened. "All, your Highness?"

"I have made answer to the gods' demands for sacrifice."

"Bad news, then, your Highness," said the other soldier. "The city mourns. The queen died while you were below. I am truly sorry. You must not have been in time."

Theseus smiled grimly. "The gods have spoken through me," he said. "And I *was* successful. I got there just in the nick of time."

♦ ♦ ♦ PERFORMING ARTS ♦ ♦ ♦

THERE WAS CRYING. THERE ALWAYS was, on the first day. "Should I stay?" asked Helen, a thin woman who vibrated with nervous energy. She looked helplessly down at her wailing child.

Diana shook her head. "She'll be fine once the lesson starts."

"Okay." Helen bent over her daughter, whose face was shiny with tears. "Darling, I have to go."

"No, Mummy!"

The teacher shooed the other mothers out the door, softly touching the girls on the head. At her touch, the girls instantly sat down on the mat, staring at the mirror on the wall without fidgeting, holding perfectly still.

Diana came back and touched Sammy on the head, too. "Twelve," the teacher said. "And I make thirteen. The perfect number." Then, to Helen, "You may leave now."

Sammy's hands dropped away from her mother. Surprised, Helen backed up towards the door, waiting for a reaction. Her daughter sat down on the mat next to the other girls, ignoring her mother as if she weren't even there.

"We'll be fine," said the teacher, pushing Helen out of the room and shutting the door in her face.

♦♦♦

Sammy's mom lingered outside the door. She had never seen her daughter so quickly listen to a stranger. Every single time at swimming class, Helen had to kneel on the edge of the concrete to convince Sammy to go into the water. Still, Sammy cried constantly.

Helen had hoped that ballet would be different, but had seen her daughter's face crumple as soon as they entered the room. For Sammy to stop crying so suddenly like that—it was strange.

Her husband always said she worried too much. *After all,* she thought, *what could be wrong with her daughter listening to the teacher?*

Nothing, of course. Absolutely nothing.

♦♦♦

When the door opened a little bit later, Sammy came running up to her mother, laughing.

"Did you have fun, darling?"

"Yes! I love Miss Diana," Sammy said.

On the car ride home, Helen heard her daughter humming something. The sound was almost tuneless, but for some reason, it made the back of Helen's neck itch.

"How about music lessons?" she suggested.

"No, Mummy. I like ballet."

♦♦♦

Between school, ballet, and other lessons, the day of the final dance recital arrived lightning-quick. The morning of the performance, Sammy was humming throughout breakfast and during the car ride to the auditorium. The sound still bothered Helen, but what could she say? She turned up the radio, but her neck still itched uncomfortably.

The place was packed. Helen's mother came up the stairs, trailing a cloud of Chanel, and kissed her on the cheek. "I'm so excited to see our little ballerina!"

The overhead lights flickered, and they found their seats. Diana walked out on the stage dressed in a black leotard and tights.

"The girls have worked very hard this season, and I think you will be surprised to see what they have put together." She bowed and the families clapped.

Out walked a line of girls. Despite the differences in height and age, there was a similarity about the girls that extended beyond the pink gauze dresses. They marched in step, forming a perfect circle without a word being said.

The audience hushed. At the head of the circle stood the teacher, like a black blot in a sea of pink. The lights went out and everyone gasped at the suddenness of the dark.

Helen strained her ears. Yes—somehow, she had expected it. A chorus of humming, gradually rising in volume. As the sound increased, the stage began to glow with light. No, that was incorrect—the dancers glowed, each with an individual spotlight. Helen glanced upwards, wondering how they were doing the lighting, but couldn't tell—the ceiling looked dark. Maybe it was coming from below.

The teacher began to speak, but not in English. The language sounded guttural, all hard stops in the back of the throat. The little girls bowed to the center of the circle with a graceful arc of their bodies. Diana raised her arms, but she did not bow. Instead, she leapt up into the air—and stayed there, hovering three feet above the ground. Helen looked for the cables holding her, but couldn't see any in the dim light. The audience applauded as each of the girls leapt after their teacher and stayed suspended.

Suddenly, the teacher broke into understandable words. "And we call you, Lord, we bid you receive this bounty we set before you."

The floor below the dancers' feet fell in with a crash. Helen found herself on her feet, shouting in panic. Before she could rush down to the stage, something came out of the hole under the dancers' feet. Something large and unimaginable, something that flowed up and over the audience in a wave.

♦♦♦

The lights came up. The dancers bowed, the stage solid beneath their pink slippers, a row of little girls flushed with the success of their first show. As if rising from a deep sleep, the members of the audience began to clap slowly. Eventually the applause grew, and the families came to their feet, cheering.

Helen shook her head. There was something she should remember. Her chest hurt, as if there was a great hollowness inside of her, something that was now gone forever. She clapped and glanced at the other parents. No one else seemed to be affected by it—the father next to her put his fingers in his mouth and whistled shrilly. Shrugging, she joined the stream of audience members heading towards the stage.

Sammy ran up to her. "Did you see? Miss Diana was right!"

"Right about what, darling?"

"We could do magic!" Sammy said.

Helen smiled tolerantly. "You certainly could, darling. Your performance was magical. I just worried at the . . . at the . . ." She rubbed at her chest, but couldn't remember what she had been about to say.

Her daughter rolled her eyes. "Oh, Mummy, sometimes you worry too much."

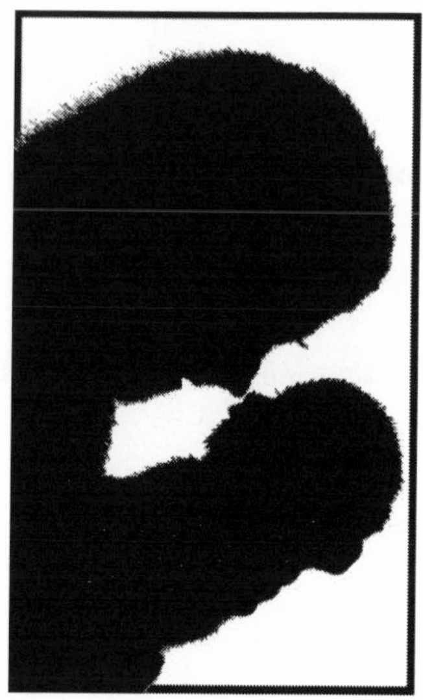

♦ ♦ ♦ THE NEXT DAY ♦ ♦ ♦

THE YETI WOMAN, NAMED SNOW, looked down at her baby boy. Held against the white fur of her arm, he looked as black as the night sky, with little flecks of silver dotting his coat like stars. So small and beautiful.

So horribly wrong.

Some time ago, her friend Walker had given birth to a baby girl with one arm. The law of the Yeti pack was clear—a week after her baby was born, her friend had made the journey down the mountain with the girl cradled in her arms. Walker had returned with the dawn, empty-handed and hollow-eyed.

Snow should make the journey, too. Tomorrow night

would be a week after her baby was born. She should abandon her distinctive baby at the edge of the human settlement to die. It was pack law.

But pack law wasn't complete. It didn't take into account the subtleties of the dilemma, all the varieties of a situation. Such as what happened after the law was followed, when she had held her friend in her arms as Walker cried for her lost child.

Snow lifted up the baby to her face and put her white, whiskery cheek against his. The baby slept on peacefully, not knowing that soon—very soon—he would be breaking his mother's heart.

♦ THE HEART OF YUKI-ONNA ♦

BEFORE FATHER'S EYES STOPPED ON her, she knew. Before he had told them that there were too many mouths to feed in winter, before her mother had fallen to the ground weeping, she knew.

"Yuki-onna," he said.

She lowered her head and nodded. Over the sound of her mother's weeping, she stood up and walked to the door. But before she opened it, she paused and half-turned back to face her family. She did not look up into the granite face of the man who had given her life—and now wanted to take it away. Instead, her eyes focused on the ground.

"Will it hurt?" she asked softly.

Her mother wailed. Her father's face, glimpsed out of the corner of her eye, seemed frozen into a mask that had no meaning. No one answered her quiet question.

She took nothing with her when she walked outside into the blizzard. She wore her kimono, but no shoes; they would be needed by the younger ones. The first touch of the snow was sharp like glass, even against her hardened soles. The winds blew through her thin kimono as if she wore nothing at all.

Staggering, she put a hand out to the cherry tree to steady herself. It was bare, as all the plants were bare, but her fingers glimpsed a hint of warmth beneath their tips, as if the tree had sympathy for her. With no other destination in mind, she sank down beneath its gentle branches and huddled upon herself.

She didn't know how long it was before the winds faded. "Yuki-onna," she heard from somewhere, and with the voice came warmth and light. She glanced up, but her lashes had frozen together and her hands didn't seem to be working properly as she tried to bat at her eyes to open them. Standing up on numb legs, there seemed to be a burning fire beneath her now. It was not unpleasant, but she longed suddenly to take off her kimono, to bathe in the waters of fire as she bathed in the meadow stream in the summer.

"Yuki-onna," she heard through the distant sounds of the storm. She reached out her hands—to what, she didn't know, as she still could see nothing through the driving snow.

There was pressure now upon her fingers, as if someone had taken them in a firm grasp. She smiled, felt herself falling slowly through the air, as if she had all the time in the world, as if each second had become a century. Her eyes were closed, but she could still see the brilliant light and feel the fires burning, burning through her until she was as light as ash. She could feel herself dissolving.

The next gust of wind picked her up and blew her away.

♦♦♦

In the morning, the storm was gone, and in its place was an unbroken ocean of white. When Hisao went outside, he knew what he would find.

But he did not find it.

Under the cherry tree, he noticed a round hollow, as if someone had lain there for a long time, but no sign of Yuki-onna. On the trunk of the tree was a perfectly white handprint, as if burned into the bark itself by a strong fire. Farther out, the fields were pristine and empty.

He went inside and told his wife. Like the night before, she fell to caterwauling until he drew back his hand and silenced her. After that, the tears dripped from her face, but she made no sound.

"She can't have gotten far," he told her. "I have better things to do than search for her."

So he did them. He chopped wood, carried in snow to melt for the cookpot. He checked his snares and was pleased to discover a rabbit in one of them. But the whole time he worked, he felt as if he were missing something. He felt as if someone were watching him, which was absurd. Yuki-onna couldn't have survived the storm. Perhaps he merely felt her dead eyes following him around from the shelter of some convenient nook where he hadn't found her body. Well, he would discover her in the springtime when the snow melted, that was for sure.

That night, Kenshin, the youngest, wouldn't stop fussing. "I want Yuki-onna!" he cried. His older sister had often let him into her warm bed at night and held him when the moaning of the wind scared him, singing lullabies. Without her, he was cold and frightened.

Hisao shouted for Kenshin to be quiet. When he wouldn't stop asking for Yuki-onna, Hisao yelled, "She is holding back the winter for us!"

Finally, the little boy stopped crying. Hisao and his wife went to sleep.

The next morning, Kenshin's bed was empty. When Hisao went tearing outside to look for his son, he found no sign of him. No trace of footprints in the snow, although no new snow had fallen since the night Yuki-onna had left. He found absolutely nothing at all.

"He must be in the house," he roared, storming inside. They looked in the cupboard, lifted up their sleeping mats, but there really weren't many places to hide.

This time, his wife was silent as she cried. But her eyes seemed to stab into him, and he could feel the gazes of his remaining children waiting for his reaction.

"I will . . . check the snares," he told them. He put on his boots and coat slowly, trying to think. When he stomped out into the snow, his feet left deep imprints, but there was no sign of any other marks. He walked in and out of the woods at the edge of the clearing, poked at the branches above his head, called out Kenshin's name. The echoes of his voice came back to him, but no sign of his younger son.

He returned home at dusk, empty-handed. His wife's eyes cut across him and his children turned away.

That night, Hisao slept fitfully. Every hour, he would start awake and go to check on his remaining three children. They had pushed their mats and blankets together and slept curled in a mess of thin, tangled limbs. His one remaining son and two daughters, all with his own coal-black eyes and their mother's rosebud mouth. His children. Near dawn, he finally fell into a deep sleep.

He walked through the woods, but the sunlight was thin and cast the ground in shadow. Snow trickled down from overhead, but the light remained constant and dim. Nothing stirred in the forest except for him—the birds were silent, the small creatures rustled no leaves and did not leap from branch to branch. Everything seemed to be hiding away, and he walked deeper into the forest with a sense of dread.

Far ahead, he glimpsed a shining white light. Sanctuary! He picked up his feet, trying to run as the wind pushed the snow into his face, as the flakes grew thicker and fell faster. He could feel the skin of his cheeks turning cold against the brutal assault of winter.

The shining ahead of him dimmed. "No!" he cried, reaching out. He pushed his legs faster, staggering in the deepening snow. The drifts were up to his ankles, his knees, his thighs. He grabbed at passing tree trunks, and the touch through his gloves raced up his arms like icicles, instantly numbing them. The white light flickered and flickered again, and he noticed that it was topped by a sea of glowing black.

Then the light grew brighter—the creature, turning. He saw that it was a woman in a white kimono, her long black hair blown back by the wind. Her lips were blue as the sky in high summer, and her coal-black eyes burned him like ice. Despite this, her face was familiar, if terrible.

He crouched down before her, bowing his head. "I am sorry, my daughter," he told the apparition.

The ghost made no answer. It reached out one long-fingered hand, the skin as white and final as death. At the last moment, he looked up and saw behind the figure the small forms of his two sons cowering behind her.

Hisao shouted, sitting upright. His wife cried out, waking up and turning to look at him. "What is it?" she demanded.

He shook his head. He didn't know what to tell her. Was it a true dream, or only a nightmare? He threw back the covers and got to his feet, although the light was still dim. He hadn't been asleep for long, perhaps only moments since the last time he'd checked on the children.

In the small house, it took only a few steps to reach their sleeping mat. He stared down at it, unbelieving.

Two children lay sleeping on the mat, their limbs entwined in sleep. His two remaining girls.

His only other son was gone.

Hisao spent a long time looking down at his sleeping daughters. His wife was sitting up on their mat now, but didn't rise to her feet. From where she was, she could see the two children. She could guess what it meant.

Still, Hisao went to the door and opened it to look out. His boot marks from the two days before were all over the white snow, but there were no other footprints. He gently closed the door, returned for his boots and coat, and went back outside without a word to his family.

His wife never knew what happened to him, for Hisao never returned. When night fell, she found a rabbit on the doorstep, frozen solid as if dipped into a vat of ice. She thawed it, skinned it and cooked it for supper, and she and her daughters ate until their stomachs were round. Every couple of days after that, there would be an offering hung on the door latch—sometimes forest creatures, sometimes cattails or baskets of nuts or piles of daikon or renkon. All the offerings were completely frozen, the nuts delivered in a basket composed of ice that melted when she put it in the stew-pot.

When spring came, the offerings ceased. But their fields sprang forth with a higher yield than they'd ever seen, and they had plenty of food set aside by the time winter returned and with only three mouths to feed. But for the rest of their lives, anytime in the winter that their supplies ran short, they would find food on their doorsteps to tide them over. The widow and her daughters became known for their generosity to others, and the village where they lived prospered. The daughters married well, and their husbands were kind to them and their children.

But, still, they never forgot their sister Yuki-onna or the day she walked out into the snow, never to return. Until the day they died, late at night when the winds moaned, they would swear they heard a voice outside singing lullabies. And once in a while, travelers through the region would stop at the village and speak about a moving light in the snow that guided them to safety in a storm. To them, the light appeared to be a woman and two small boys, glowing with a shine as beautiful and serene as the moon.

Stories from *Enchantress of Books* have previously been published in:

Abbreviated Epics Anthology

Broadswords and Blasters

Double Take Anthology

EGM Shorts

Enchanted Conversation

Fantasia Divinity Magazine

Fundamentally Challenged: Stories of Possible People and Impossible Change Anthology

Halloween Forevermore

Mystic Signals

On the Premises

Once Upon a Scream Anthology

Swords and Sorcery Magazine

Tales from the Sunrise Lands Anthology

The Lorelei Signal

Up and Coming: Stories by the 2016 Campbell Eligible Authors Anthology

About the Cover Artist

Richard Ong is a multi-talented Renaissance man whose stories, poetry, artwork, and photos have appeared in several issues of *Bewildering Stories*, *Foliate Oak Literary Magazine* and *Yesterday's Magazette*. He is also one of the executive producers of short film "Angelics: Ascension" (2018) available for viewing at Amazon Prime Video.

His non-genre-based literary work has appeared in print in two anthologies—*Toys Remembered* (2011) and "Serendipity" (2015), both of which are available in Amazon and Barnes & Noble. Not wanting to limit himself in individual publishing endeavors, Richard has also worked closely with the curator and senior staff of Toronto's Gibson House Museum to create a pictorial story album titled, "The Gibsons—Prudence's Story" (available in iBooks and Blurb 2015), giving the reader a virtual tour of the historic building.

Richard has over a hundred published artworks online, in which the original projects were done using a wide range of tools such as digital, acrylic and mixed media. In his (much) younger days, Richard's reckless spirit of adventure once took him everywhere, from rock climbing off a limestone quarry, glacier hiking in Iceland, freezing at -54 degrees Celsius in Yellowknife to photograph the Aurora Borealis, kayaking through small chunk icebergs and playful humpback whales off the coast of Newfoundland, and onboard a high performance jet fighter in St. Petersburg, FL.

Email: richardong@sympatico.ca

Other Contributing Artists

Most of the pictures for the stories are thanks to the talented artists who have listed their work on the website https://pixabay.com. A number of their images were further enhanced/modified by me to fit the stories, but the original creative talent belongs to the artists.

While many of the artists on Pixabay go by online pseudonyms, I'd like to give a shout-out to the artists whose names are listed with the images that were used.

Gerd Altmann – Images associated with "Enchantress of Books" and the image for the collection's back cover.

Gordon Johnson – Image associated with "Grandmother Winter."

Alexandra Haynak – Image associated with "The Godmother's Bargain."

Mohamed Hassan – Images associated with "After War" and "The Lost Children."

Sy-Jei-Vee – Image associated with "A Farmer's Good Luck."

A hearty thank you to all these fabulous artists!

About the Author

Diversity is one of Alison McBain's passions. With dual Canadian-U.S. citizenship, a Japanese-American mother and a B.A. in African history and classical literature, she has an eclectic background and a wide range of experience. She grew up in California and moved to the East Coast in her mid-twenties, finally settling in Connecticut to raise her three daughters.

She started her writing career at age four with a "self-published" horror story about the monster in the closet. The story was highly lauded by her closest family members. Since then, she's received a number of writing awards and accolades from people not even vaguely related to her, but she still has a soft spot for that first short story.

Her interest in diversity also extends to fiction. With nearly a hundred short publications to her name, her stories and poems range in tone from serious to silly. Her work covers nearly every genre, including literary, romance, horror, science fiction, fantasy, history and adventure. Her debut fantasy novel *The Rose Queen*, a YA retelling of beauty and the beast, was published in July 2018. She was also the lead editor of *When to Now: A Time Travel Anthology*, published in October 2018. A recent nominee for the prestigious Pushcart Prize award, her fiction has also been honored with the Patricia McFarland Memorial Award, the quarterly award at *Bewildering Stories*, and received honorable mention for the Roswell Award.

When not writing fiction, she follows her own personal mantra of, "Do something creative every day." She serves as the Book Reviews Editor at the magazine *Bewildering Stories*. She also blogs about local events, showcases her art and conducts author interviews on her website, http://www.alisonmcbain.com/. When life gets a little too hectic, she does origami meditation or draws all over the walls of her house with the enthusiastic help of her kids.

42520780R00125

Made in the USA
Middletown, DE
16 April 2019